GUARDING GABLE

A Novel by

NAT SEGALOFF

GUARDING GABLE

A Novel by

NAT SEGALOFF

Bear Manor Media
2019

Published by Bear Manor Media
and printed in the United States of America
www.BearManorMedia.com

ISBN 978-1-62933-406-6 (paperback)
ISBN 978-1-62933-407-3 (hardcover)

Many of the designations used by manufacturers to distinguish their products are claimed as trademarks or service marks such as Oscar®, Academy Award®, and SPAM® Luncheon Meat. Where those designations appear, and the author and publisher were aware of such a claim, the designations contain the symbols ®, ℠, or ™ on their initial appearance. Any omission of these symbols is purely accidental and is not intended as infringement.

Cover photo courtesy of DL Guss, Fine Art America (www.fineartamerica.com). Other photographs are from Wiki Commons and are deemed to be in the Public Domain. Those believing their photograph has been used in error should contact the publisher with proof of ownership and the image will be deleted from future editions.

Author's acknowledgments: It is only because of Nikki Finke's enthusiasm and support that this book is seeing paper and pixels. I owe her more than I can say, not only for her graciousness with this book but for publishing me on her website www.HollywoodDementia.com. Michael Sugar and J.B. Sugar provided early guidance polishing my original material. Since then, I received encouragement from Yoram Ben-Ami, Agnes Birnbaum, Christopher Darling, Susan Feiles, Barry Krost, Rochelle O'Gorman, Melanie Ruth Rose, and Dorla Salling, for which I am grateful. I also wish to thank producer David Ladd for his kind words at a time when he didn't know how much I needed them.

Cover & Book design by Darlene Swanson • van-garde.com

Dedication:

THIS BOOK IS RESPECTFULLY dedicated to the members of the 351st Bombardment Group of the U.S. Army Air Forces stationed in England during World War Two and, in particular, to cameraman Andrew J. McIntyre, whose devotion to both America and MGM inspired this story.

AUTHOR'S NOTE:

Surprisingly, much of what follows is true.

Chapter 1

THE KING PACED HIS throne room with deeply un-royal anxiety. He longed for his queen with a passion known only to royals, or so the fairy tales say. Since their celebrated marriage barely twenty months earlier, the two of them had been out of each other's sight only when affairs of State commanded their separation. For the past fortnight, the King had been compelled by royal obligation to remain within easy traveling distance of the castle while his Queen journeyed to the far heartland of their realm on a mission of great diplomacy and urgency.

For there was a great war. The kingdom was being attacked by forces of evil, and the King and Queen had drawn their country together in spirit even as the details of fighting that war tore the royal couple apart.

The Queen missed her King with equal fire. The duty that took her away was a personal appearance at a rally to raise money for the war effort. January 16, 1942 was just five weeks into the war. Already the kingdom was unified through a well-run campaign of public support and patriotism. The entire court had been dispatched to crisscross the country bolstering unanimity and asking the citizenry to pay money in addition to their taxes in order to keep their nation alive and stave off the collapse of the free world.

The Queen's mission took her to the town of Indianapolis in the state of Indiana. Her appearance drew thousands of people and, as she ended her impassioned speech, she told them all, "In leaving you now, I want you all to join me in raising your hands in making the sign of victory — the 'V' sign popularized by our famous ally across the sea, Winston Churchill. Heads and hands up, America. Let's give a rousing cheer that'll be heard in Berlin and Tokyo. C'mon! Hooray!"

They cheered with the last of their breath and emptied the last of their purses at the Queen's behest. Climbing weakly down the unpolished wooden steps from the hastily constructed stage, she turned to her friend and courtier, Otto Winkler, and asked, "Do we have the plane tickets yet?"

"Almost," said Winkler, who, in addition to his friendship, was in charge of her public relations. "TWA Flight Three'll take us back to Burbank. They're confirming now. Are you sure you want to fly?"

"What the matter?" asked the blond regent with the mixture of charm and sass that had endeared her to millions, "You chicken?"

"Yes," Otto stated flatly. "Both your mother and I don't want to fly. We've got train reservations, why not take that? Trains don't fall out of the sky."

"But planes are faster," she said, "and Clark is waiting."

She didn't have to say it. Everyone knew. She and the King had been an item even before they married, but since their union had become official, what belonged to one belonged to the other, including their retinues. Technically, Otto belonged to the King, but he was pleased to be seconded to his Queen and surrendered to her charm. "Okay," he sighed. "Are you all packed?"

"I've never had the chance to unpack during this whole goddamn schlep," the Queen smiled, or tried to smile, through her exhaustion. Nobody took her profanity seriously. When she really let it fly, she hit home, but casual swearing was as natural to her as an affectionate pat on the back, which Otto took this to be. He marveled at her fortitude and noted that it was entirely in keeping with her indomitable character.

"Anyway," he reasoned, "you can sleep on the plane. It's only eighteen hours."

"Eighteen hours from here to Burbank?" questioned Elizabeth Peters, the Queen's mother. "I could thumb a ride faster on Route 66."

Otto was prepared with the airline itinerary. "Flight three bounces in St. Louis, Albuquerque, Las Vegas, and God knows where else. Then it's over the Rockies and finally into Burbank."

"That's what I call a milk run," said the Queen. "Is there any way to land sooner?"

"We could set her down in the Grand Canyon," Otto joked. "Any more bright ideas?" He was respectful but never sycophantic.

As the small royal group was hustled into the limousine that would take them to the hotel, and then to the airport, a uniformed woman urgently rushed to them. "We just got a tally, Mr. Winkler," the woman said. "Miss Lombard raised two million dollars today. That's a record."

"It's just the start," Carole responded. "As soon as I can get my lazy-ass husband to go out on the road with me, we'll beat Hitler with a checkbook."

The uniformed woman's face froze. She wasn't sure whether to laugh at Lombard's wisecrack or take offense at its vulgarity. Or maybe she was mulling the possibility of meeting the Queen's husband sometime down the road."

"Thank you, soldier," Winkler said. "I'm sure Jimmie Fiddler and the other columnists will be as overjoyed as we are to learn that. We'll take the opportunity of telling them so you won't have to bother. Thanks for the swell send-off."

On the way back to the hotel, a stern-looking Mrs. Peters turned to her daughter. "You can't talk like that," she lectured the star. "This isn't one of your studio crews that knows you. This is your public."

"Talk like what?" Carole said, the picture of innocence.

"'Lazy-ass husband,'" her mother repeated. "You can tell any of us that Clark is your lazy-ass husband because we all know he isn't, and we also know that it's a joke. But suppose some local reporter asks that girl what you said to her? It'll be in all the papers. Otto, say something."

Winkler's thoughts were elsewhere. Even though the free-spirited Lombard wasn't an MGM star, the studio had attached Winkler to her bond tour to run interference. He was Clark Gable's personal publicist, and they were friends, and Gable knew Carol would be in good hands. Back in Culver City, Gable was still shooting "*Somewhere I'll Find You*," and the studio's publicity chief, Howard Strickling, was ever-vigilant about Lombard's loose lips. As much as he admired her spunk, he cringed at her lack of discretion and didn't want any of her zingers to compromise his own press work for Gable. Otto was weighing whether to tell Strickling about Carole's gaffe or wait to see what appeared in print. He was confident that no family newspaper would print such a vulgarism, but the Hollywood gossip mill was something else. It would wait.

The Douglas DC3-382 "Skycub" prop-liner was scheduled to arrive from New York in time for a 4 AM departure from Indianapolis. Lombard, Peters, Winkler, and their party joined the passengers who were already aboard the transcontinental flight under the piloting of 41-year-old Captain Wayne C. Williams.

If Williams had any foreknowledge of his illustrious passenger list, it would not have impressed him. The New York-to-LA run was old hat as far as he was concerned, and celebrities had been turning from train to air travel ever since it had been commercially offered in 1934. Williams had been with TWA since 1931 and had logged thousands of hours for them, many at the controls of the DC-3. There was one curious asterisk on his record, however; in 1933 he had been fired for changing his flight plan without authorization. He had been reinstated after a hearing, and thereafter stuck to the rules.

The flight, though prestigious, was nevertheless a physical ordeal. It could take up to 24 hours — more if the weather interfered and caused layovers. Many people still preferred the train which, while slower, at least afforded them comfort. In addition, movie stars took the train when they wanted to get noticed; the press routinely haunted the Pasadena railroad station looking for celebrities, and the celebrities routinely obliged with a smile and a wave from the end of the Pullman car. It was an honorable bargain: their faces sold papers, the papers sold their faces. In an era when each of Los Angeles's half-dozen papers put out several editions a day, by the time the train chugged from Pasadena into downtown Union Station, the extra would be on the streets touting the celebrity's arrival.

But publicity wasn't on Carole's mind, She wanted to be back in Clark's arms—or, more specifically, his bed— and the plane was mightier than the train.

Flight TWA-3 took off as scheduled from Indianapolis and made its wee-hours stops along the way, including Albuquerque, New Mexico. When they landed there, the Station Agent boarded the plane and introduced himself.

"I'm sorry to inconvenience you," he told the groggy passengers, "but I'm afraid I need to requisition your seats."

"What's the problem?" Otto stepped in.

"No problem, sir," the Station Agent said, "but we have several servicemen who have to get back to Los Angeles and, under War Department rules, they are allowed to displace civilians on commercial flights like this."

"Do you know who this woman is?" asked Bess Peters, nodding toward her daughter.

"Yes," the Station Agent said. "I'm sorry, Miss Lombard, but there's a war on."

"A war is what I just raised two million dollars to fight," the actress said politely but firmly. "Doesn't that count for anything?"

Before the Station Agent could answer, Otto Winkler offered, "Miss Lombard is as crucial to the war effort, in her way, as these soldiers are in theirs. I should think that the War Department would understand allowing us to continue."

"But, sir," the Station Agent attempted.

"Meaning no disrespect," Otto continued in his business voice, "let me put it another way. You can call the War Department or MGM can call the War Department and we'll see who gets through first."

It was no contest. "Very well, sir," the Station Agent said. "But I'll have to ask the other civilian passengers to deplane." They did without complaint, casting tolerant glances at Carole as they left, and were replaced by an equal number of servicemen. Once airborne, Carole greeted each of the newly seated soldiers and tried to raise their morale as the plane headed west.

In the interest of speed, Captain Williams skipped an optional refueling stop in Winslow, Arizona, and proceeded directly to Las Vegas for refueling. There they also changed the flight attendant and co-pilot.

At 7 PM the flight resumed from Las Vegas Airport. Preparing to over-fly the mountains, Williams switched on the extra oxygen supply to help the passengers breathe more easily in the thinning air, even though the cabin was pressurized.

Carole tried to nap. She wanted to be alert and fresh when she saw Clark again. As usual when either of them went out of town, one would wait at the terminal for the other. The "A" sticker in their car windshields gave them enough gasoline for such pleasantries even in the face of wartime rationing. Such was the privilege of fame.

The flight gained altitude. It yawed slightly in the updrafts that blew up from the mountains. It was too dark to find the skyline through the windows, and there were no city lights to be seen from the sparsely settled land at the base of Potosi Mountain. They leveled at 7,770 feet when the aircraft, its fuel, and all souls aboard slammed nose-first without warning into the side of the mountain.

Another eighty feet and they would have cleared the peak.

The aircraft was going at two hundred miles an hour when its fuel tanks, still freshly filled from the Las Vegas airport, exploded on impact. The shattering fuselage rapelled off the steep cliff, accelerated by the fireball, and splayed over the broad mountain. The cold January weather had brought a snowfall that cushioned the sound of falling debris, which included body parts from Lombard, Winkler, Peters, pilot Williams, two crew members, and the sixteen other passengers and service men who died in an instant of history.

When Flight 3 failed to contact the control tower at Burbank Airport, officials feared the worst.

Clark Gable, waiting at the Lockheed terminal to greet Lombard, heard the mumbled conversation of gate personnel and approached them to ask if there was some kind of trouble. When told that Lombard's flight was missing, he immediately chartered a plane for Las Vegas.

Chapter 2

CLARK GABLE WASTED NO time on pleasantries. "Let's get out there," he told the Las Vegas police when they met him at the airport.

"I can't let you go to the crash site, Mr. Gable," said the officer in charge. "It's almost at the crest of the mountain. There aren't even any trails. We have a search party already working their way up there."

"Don't tell me what I can and can't do," Gable — the King of Hollywood — said softly but sternly. "Even if Ma's dead, I want to see her." There was no stopping the King. He drove to the base of the mountain and sprang from the car, heading up the slope with attendants and press trailing.

Potosi, only thirty miles from Las Vegas, was foreboding beneath the snow, a rough landscape strewn with stones and cactus, but nothing green. Even plants hated being there. A rescue party had already been formed by Jack Moore and Lyle Van Gordon, and they had struggled to reach the crash site. Behind them crawled news photographers, climbing over one another to grab pictures of Gable.

As January 17 broke over the craggy skyline, it found Gable recklessly tossing rocks aside looking the faintest first sign of the tragedy. No one dared tell him that searchers had already brought Lombard's body down the snow incline. It had been found without her head.

Finally Gable stopped. Something ahead caught his eye. Others noticed and closed around him, trying to restrain the six-foot-one, physically fit actor who was only two weeks away from his forty-first birthday. Gable broke free and rushed to pick up what he had seen, but then he paused halfway there, realizing that, as much as he wanted to find Carole, he did not want to find this. Instead, one of the searchers fetched the object and wordlessly handed it to him. Nothing needed to be said. He put it in his pocket.

"All right, boys," he said. "Let's go back to town and let the rescue team do their job."

By the time he returned to the airport, Metro-Goldwyn-Mayer's publicity team was in control. Publicity chief Howard Strickling, given carte blanche above his already limitless powers by studio operations manager Eddie Mannix, was simultaneously making funeral arrangements and managing press access. The press, eager to grab photos of a shocked Gable, also knew where their publishers' bread was buttered and pretended to respect the King's grief even as they snapped for the archive. Strickling hustled the star into a studio limo and took off for the Gables' Palm Springs home at 222 W. Chino Drive in the Old Las Palmas neighborhood. Before leaving, he phoned Culver City to spread word to assemble the studio publicity department in the Gable living room and wait for them to arrive.

MGM's limousines were reserved for company executives, important exhibitors, and visiting politicians. Like the Gable coupe, they were given federal dispensation to buy gas and tires during the war. On world premieres, they would form rotating fleets to escort the stars and directors to the red carpet. They were outfitted with mirrors and lighting (to check makeup), slant boards instead of seats (so as not to wrinkle gowns), and a full wet bar. It was that latter service that Gable began hitting on the long drive home. By the time he reached his front door, he had to be helped inside by Strickling. Even though he had not slept all night, Gable passed up the bedroom and headed straight for his den, which had its own wet bar. And something more important: solitude.

Strickling left him there, shook his head in sorrow (for he loved Carole, too; everybody did), and joined his fellow publicists in the living room.

"We'll leave him alone for now," Strickling said paternally. He looked around the room at his staff and filled them in on what he knew. Their faces, normally immune to the craziness of Hollywood news, melted into shock.

"The papers already grilled us as we came in, Howard," one of them said. "What more can we tell them that the wire services and the Vegas police haven't already released?"

Strickling parted the curtains to see for himself and was greeted with a flash in the face from a Graflex camera.

"Let's not let this get out of control," he said, rubbing his eyes. "We don't report on the crash. That's old news. We show how the studio is united behind Clark, all of us supporting Clark and the public in their grief. Sandy, take this down, would you?" The young woman, already dressed and made up for work, unfolded her steno pad. "The entire Metro-Goldwyn-Mayer family joins Clark Gable in his private grief," he dictated, glancing down the hall to where the King was sequestered. "Miss Lombard gave her life to the war effort and, in her memory, MGM has committed itself to buying ten thousand dollars in 1942 Series war bonds in her name and in her honor."

Sandy looked up from her writing. "Ten thousand, as in ten thousand U.S. dollars?"

"Don't worry," Strickling said, "we'll hide it in the budget for Clark's next picture." Sandy looked around the room to see if anyone else was as surprised as she was at Strickling's callousness. She was new here.

The phone rang and someone picked it up. "Telephone call for you, Howard."

"Not now!" he barked.

"It's Mr. Mayer."

Strickling immediately took the phone and huddled into a wall niche for privacy.

"Yes, L.B." he said to the head of the studio. Strickling didn't sound obsequious, but he didn't sound over-confident, either. Louis B. Mayer could be mercurial, which is a polite way of saying that he could spin off the handle, even becoming physical, at the slightest provocation.

"Yes, he's drinking." Another pause. "Well, besides Carole, there was her mother, Bess Peters, and the crew and servicemen. And of coursed Otto. Otto Winkler, from my — your — publicity department. He's the only one Clark ever trusted. Yes, sir, I'm issuing a press release to that effect and saying that MGM will buy ten thousand dollars' worth of war bonds in Carole's name. Yes, sir. I'll get back to you when anything breaks."

Strickling hung up and walked to where Sandy was typing the press release. "Hold on a second with that," he said. Sandy stopped typing. "Cut it to five thousand," Strickling said and walked back to the living room.

"All right, everyone," he commanded, "from now on until further notice we are all in the Clark Gable business. Starting with the funeral on Thursday, everything we do helps Clark deal with this tragedy." Then he added, speaking more softly, "and gets him back to work."

Strickling, whose cleverness and political acumen—as was his long memory and skill in using it for leverage—was legendary. It was he who shielded the studio and its contract personnel with a web of favors and intrigues, and when those failed, bribes did the trick. When Paul Bern, Jean Harlow's new husband, shot himself and left a cryptic note behind, Stickling stepped in. Mayer himself had pocketed the note, not wanting the police to get a taste of the scandal, until Strickling advised his boss not to withhold evidence. The note, in which Bern confessed to the "wrong I have done you and to wipe out my abject humiliation," became public and for years the legend persisted that he had taken his own life after finding that he couldn't sexually satisfy the screen's reigning sex goddess. In fact, shortly after his marriage to Harlow, Bern's common law wife showed up threatening criminal and civil action. The fact that Strickling preferred Bern, who had been a friend, to be thought of as a eunuch rather than a bigamist speaks volumes, but underscores his protectiveness toward MGM. Now he was turning that talent to helping the biggest star in the world. Like a general, which, in a way, he was, he tasked each publicist with a specific job. "Harry, keep working on the funeral arrangements. Give it class, and make sure the press uses the word *class* when they cover it. Sylvia—flowers. Carole loved flowers. Josh, you and Brad set up the seating chart for the chapel at Forest Lawn. Look at where we sat people when we planted Thalberg."

"Can we do that, Howard?" Josh said. "I checked our file copy of Carole's Last Will and she said she wanted only immediate family in the case of her death."

"And she wants to be buried next to her mother," Brad added. "Do you think we ought to try to get around it?"

"All of Metro is her immediate family!" Strickling pronounced, then thought better. "Okay, we won't do anything that might anger Clark. Look, send flowers to the cemetery and we'll plan a separate memorial on Stage Nineteen when the time is right. Good thing you caught that, Josh."

"Another press wagon just rolled up," Harry reported, glancing out the window. "Looks like a premiere out there."

"Shit," Strickling said. "Harry, call the cops. Tell 'em we've got a potential riot outside the Gable retreat and tell 'em to give 'em the bum's rush. Then, as soon as they start, I'll run out and tell 'em to leave the boys alone. Who's got the fan magazine list? Agnes?"

"Yes, Mr. Strickling," answered the prim Agnes. "We were about to put out a spread on Clark's upcoming picture, *Somewhere I'll Find You*. Should I put a stop on it?"

"Not on your life. Just say that production is being suspended and we'll resume as soon as Mr. Gable feels he's ready. He's a pro and respects a contract. But, hey, let's float the idea of re-releasing *Honky Tonk* next week. Maybe we can squeeze a few more bucks out of it. No use wasting all that ink on just a funeral." He started to leave the room to check on Gable when he turned and said in his first sincere voice of the day, "Oh, and let's get a collection going for Otto's widow."

As he left, his eyes fell on a young publicist who was struggling to pry a photograph of Gable and Lombard out of a silver frame on the mantelpiece. He had been watching him while speaking of Otto's fund, but now became fascinated with the young man's efforts. "What in hell are you doing?" Stirckling finally asked.

The young man ignored the question until he could answer it by holding up the picture. "We need a two-shot of Clark and Carole for the papers. Nothing in our files is any good. This'll do."

"*You're stealing it from the house of mourning?*" Strickling was incredulous at the gall.

"We need it," the kid said. "If we don't take it, one of the press will."

"*Who are you?*" Stickling asked in full italics.

"Alan Greenberg" I said.

"Are you with the publicity department?"

I nodded Yes.

"*My* publicity department?"

Another nod. Strickling turned to address the room. "Does anyone here know what this young man does for us?"

No one did. He leaned over and forced himself close enough to me to breathe up my nostrils. "Okay, I give up. Whose relative are you?"

"No one's, sir. I was hired as a junior publicist fresh out of high school. I work in the stills department."

"Greenstein, is it?"

"Greenberg."

He put his hand on my shoulder, squeezed, and said, "Wait here." Then he turned to the group. "Okay, everyone, you all know what to do. Now go and do it for Clark, for Mr. Mayer, and for MGM." Then he turned to me. "Good thinking on the picture," and left the room to check on Gable. No one else moved. They were all staring at me. I couldn't tell if they were offended, impressed, or saw me as competition now that I had Howard Strickling's warm handprint on my body.

I'd felt their steely eyes on me ever since I'd started working in the deepest basement of the studio's publicity building, but nobody had said anything. You can't be sure. In Hollywood, you never know if the person you want to stab in the back is somebody's relative. Now I had not only announced myself as a pilferer, but as a nepotistic orphan ripe for stabbing, gutting, and removal from the Metro jungle.

Here is where I join the Gable story in progress. I will tell it as best I remember, but you have to grant me dispensation for all the years since it took place, all the time I have waited before writing it down, and all the scores I intend to settle along the way.

Chapter 3

EVEN THOUGH MR. MAYER insisted that MGM was one big family, he never let us play together like one. The studio might have had more stars than there were in heaven, but it was made clear to all of us that not all stars were of the same magnitude. The "A" stars such as Spencer Tracy, Katharine Hepburn, Judy Garland, Fred Astaire, Gene Kelly, Greer Garson, and, of course Clark Gable, would not mix on the lot with "B" stars like Angela Lansbury, Lew Ayres, Lewis Stone, J. Carol Naish, June Allyson, or Faye Bainter. "B" stars might play supporting roles in "A" moves, but never the other way around. They might nod to them in the commissary, but never sit together. It was like high school, with money.

By the same token, those of us pushing pencils, props, or dollies on the lot would never dare to start a conversation with an actor unless we were assigned to serve him or her. Even then, the introduction had an expiration date; you could only say hello to one of the stars for up to six months after working with them. It wasn't that they were haughty, it was that they met so many people that you never wanted to embarrass them by thinking that they would remember you.

Some jobs were allowed more familiarity than others. Hair, make-up, and costuming were of an intimate nature and produced closer bonds than writing, set dressing, or (ahem) publicity. Howard Strickling was the only publicist allowed close contact with the people whose names we all kept in the papers, and sometimes out. The rest of us merely did his bidding, ladder rung by ladder rung.

I was on the bottom. Invisible. Among the advantages of being invisible is that people don't see you and, like the nobles treat their servants, feel that they can talk freely around them. Whether I was trusted or wasn't even worth considering quickly came to matter little to me. The point was that I remembered.

It was luck that led me to MGM. I had wanted to be a journalist, inspired by the vivid writing of the New York papers that I read growing up in the Boroughs. But when I saw that, with the coming of sound, all the good newspaper writers seemed to migrate to Hollywood to write for the talkies, I decided to try that, too. Alas, running into Herman Mankiewicz, Ben Hecht, Charles MacArthur, Gene Fowler, or Frank Nugent, among others, wasn't going to happen to Alan Greenberg whose diploma from PS 84 stressed writing and nothing else. So I thumbed out on my own, got a cheap room, scoured the newspaper ads for "Help Wanted—Male," and landed an entry level job at Metro. That was in 1940. Then came World War Two and Carole Lombard's death..

At the Gable home the morning after returning from the crash site, Howard Strickling cracked the door of the den and tried to see into the dim, smoke-hazy light. "Clark, it's Howard." Hearing only heavy breathing and the clink of ice in a highball glass, Strickling entered and shut the heavy door behind him.

Gable's den was an outdoorsman's sanctuary. Wood floor with deep-pile area rugs, paneled ceiling, and real wood-paneled walls hung with trophy heads of the animals that the King had claimed on hunting trips. No movie memorabilia for him; this room was as far away from movies as Gable could get, and it was here that he came when he needed to escape from his job's interminable make-believe. He'd long since accepted acting as a profession that was, if not exactly noble, then at least not effeminate or seditious. Winning the Academy Award® for *It Happened One Night* in 1934 and losing one for *Gone With the Wind* five years later had taught him how quirky fame could be, so he resolved to ignore it and concentrate on living life. Marrying Carole on March 29, 1939 renewed his interest in living after two disastrous marriages. The first, to Josephine Dillon, lasted from December 13, 1924 to April 1, 1930. He was just shy of 24 when he married the older Dillon, who capped his teeth, nurtured his early career, and then became possessive. They divorced and, on July 19, 1931 he married Maria Franklin Langham. It was an increasingly uneasy alliance, marred by his fathering a daughter by Loretta Young, with whom he co-starred in the 1935 picture, *Call of the Wild*. I'd always thought that Loretta Young was more pious than she had any right to be, and when news of her illegitimate child finally broke through the barrier of discretion, I was happy that the daughter was given an identity and smugly justified about her mother's hypocrisy. In 1936 Gable and Lombard began seeing each other, and it took three years before Maria agreed to call it quits with Clark. She and Gable divorced on March 4, 1939 and twenty-five days later Clark and Carole tied the knot that was meant to last forever, not just a lifetime.

What impressed everybody was how Carole kept up with Clark. It wasn't easy. He was a highly active outdoorsman, and she might not have liked hunting and fishing and camping, but, by God, she did it to please him, and they were a team.

Now she was gone, and Gable was inconsolable. Strickling ventured closer to the easy chair where the King had dropped and from which he had not moved except to empty more of a whiskey decanter into his glass.

"We're all worried about you, Clark," Howard said tentatively.

"We?" Gable grunted.

"L.B. — Eddie Mannix — me — your whole MGM family."

"Well, stop," he said. "I got it all figured out."

Strickling froze. He was used to actors being melodramatic, but not Gable. "You're not gonna do anything stupid, are you?"

"Nah. Ma wouldn't like that."

"What is it, then, Clark? C'mon, you can trust me."

Gable took another drink. He knew better than to trust Strickling. Otto was the only one. When the silence continued, Strickling prompted, "Tell me what's on your mind, Clark. You know that L.B. doesn't like surprises."

Gable leaned forward into the light, looked up at Strickling, and did that half-laugh that let you know he was riding a private joke, and said, "Fuck L.B."

The King was shitfaced.

Strickling couldn't get a thing out of him, not by playing confidante, not by invoking the name of Loew's president Nick Schenck, and not by outright begging. He even played the work card: "Maybe if you went back to shooting your picture you could distract yourself."

"Nuts," said the King. "No way in hell am I going to step onto a set to make a picture called *Somewhere I'll Find You.* For starters, change the title."

"I'll tell them," Strickling said, thinking he had made inroads until Gable said, "I'll think about it. Now leave me alone."

He poured himself another drink. The ice had melted in the one he had been nursing, but he didn't get up to refill it. Strickling realized that there was nothing else he could do here except stay in the house, wanted or unwanted, until the King called out for him. He was used to this. He'd lost count of how many times Metro's stars had told him they hated his guts, but who was the first person they called when they were in trouble? As Strickling closed the door of the den, he heard Gable saying, into his glass, "Whatever you say, Ma. What's that? Oh, sure, I'll tell him. Fuck L.B."

Chapter 4

"ENLIST?!?"

Louis B. Mayer could have broken his oak desk in half if he had brought his fist down as hard as he screamed at Strickling, who told him the news, and Eddie Mannix, who had heard it first.

"He wants to do his patriotic duty," Strickling tried explaining. Mayer was having none of it.

"He can do that on Stage twenty-seven. When do we wrap *Somewhere I'll Find You?*"

"February 23," Mannix said. "Then there's reshoots and pickups."

"The sonofabitch is really going to enlist?" Mayer repeated disbelievingly.

"Not only that," Strickling continued carefully, "he said 'I'm going in and I don't expect to come back and I don't give a hoot if I do or not.'"

"He's talking suicide," Mannix, a bulldog of a man, said sternly.

"No!" shouted Mayer. "He's talking murder! He's gonna kill us. Eddie, find a way to stop him."

"I'll keep him under watch, L.B.," Mannix said, searching for something better to say, "but how do you stop Clark Gable from doing anything?"

"Get him arrested for something! You've done it before for other people." Mayer was now at a level six panic mode.

Stickling picked up Mannix' desperate mood. "Maybe we can turn this into a public relations windfall — you know, when war comes, kings go forth."

Mannix suddenly took Mayer's side. "Save the flag-waving for L.B.'s birthday parade. We've got a star with a death wish. You remember Barrymore. Wally Beery. Tracy when he's in his cups. You and I get the same phone calls at three in the morning from the Beverly Hills Police."

Both men turned to Mayer. Powerfully built, bespectacled and with an owlish look that seemed far off but could burn through men's souls, L.B. calmed himself down. "It's settled," he pronounced. "Gable doesn't enlist. This year the exhibitors are expecting a Hepburn, a Van Johnson, a Greer Garson, two Thin Mans, two Andy Hardy's, and two Gables. Y'hear? Two Gables—one of which has wrapped late and another that we're in pre-production on. What's he thinking?"

"He's just lost his wife, L.B," Mannix said gently. "Don't the goyum have a period of mourning?"

"Not this long," Mayer said. "I already asked three priests and the Bishop."

"I'll get him to change his mind when the time is right," Stickling said. "Leave it to me."

"It's too late for that," Mayer said, picking up the phone, "not if he's got his heart set on enlisting." He pressed the call button on his desk intercom. "Get me President Roosevelt."

Stickling and Mannix looked at each other, puzzled.

"I'll get him to do me a favor," Mayer said with a conspiratorial twinkle in his eyes.

"But L.B., you *hate* FDR. You called the New Deal a Communist plot."

"It is," Mayer said, waiting for the call to go through.

"You're the chief fundraiser for Hollywood's Republican party."

"I am! And after Roosevelt does me this one little favor, I'll go back to hating him again. You happy?"

Neither man had a response that sounded any less ludicrous. In their silence, Mayer's secretary buzzed. "Mr. Mayer, the White House says they'll have to call you back. They say the President is busy with World War Two."

This time Mayer did slam his desk with his meaty fist. "God damn it, who does he think he is?"

I didn't hear the desk noise all the way down in the publicity department, halfway across the lot from Mayer's tirade, but I swear I felt the ground tremble, although it could also have been a small earthquake. They were often the same. Mr. Strickling seldom came down to this end of the building, and the stars most certainly never did, even though we worked ten hours a day on their behalf.

My job was considered entry-level, but that was a misnomer because, in practice, it was the one that sent most people exiting the company, many of them screaming. It was my tedious task to log the fan letters and send out the autographed photos. We kept track of the number of letters that our stars received, not to make them feel good, but to give our business affairs people leverage at contract renewal time. I must confess to fudging the amounts for stars whose work I liked, but I never withheld counts for any that I had problems with. I might have been corrupt, but I was honest about it.

I had languished in nameless obscurity before being outed at the Gable home, but now that I was known to my colleagues, any languishing was over. I was the publicity department's Cinderella. "Greenberg!" someone like Josh or Harry would call out, "I need a Van Johnson and a Judy Garland" And I would oblige. I did not do this by pestering Van or Judy while they were between takes or resting in their dressing rooms. No, when a senior publicist like Josh or Harry asked for a signed photo, it meant that they were doing a favor for someone important, someone who had done something to benefit the studio. In such cases, I went to the card file, took out the sample signature of the requested star, and signed their name on the photograph.

Forgery is such an ugly word. I prefer *facsimile*. The more popular the star, the higher the demand for signed photos, and the less often I needed to refer to the sample. With the really big ones, I got so that I could just do it. It would have made for a good party trick if I had ever been invited to those kind of parties.

Gable received so many fan letters that I got good at doing "Kind regards, Clark Gable." Not every piece of fan mail was a photo request, and some were not on paper. The week after Carole's death, Gable received over five thousand condolences, four marriage proposals, twenty bibles, and three sets of underwear, two of them from women. It was my job to answer everything but the underwear.

While this was going on in the publicity pit, Mr. Mayer was trying to strike a deal with President Roosevelt.

"Clark Gable is a national treasure, Mr. President," he campaigned. "He's the biggest movie star in the world. He's also forty-one. You don't take men that old, do you? Oh, you do?"

L.B. changed his tactics, no doubt realizing that he was trying to con one of the greatest con men who ever sat in the Oval Office.

"I'm not asking for anything you haven't done for others," Mayer continued. "You're keeping John Wayne and Ronald Reagan out of combat, aren't you?" Mr. Mayer's face dropped and he covered the mouthpiece to tell Mannix, "He says that's because they didn't want to go." Immediately he snapped back on the line, "What's that, Mr. President? But what does that have to do with — oh, I see. Yes, sir, I'll look into it. Not at all, sir. And my regards to Mrs. Roosevelt."

Apparently FDR had been forewarned about Mayer's call. He had Gable's enlistment papers in front of him; Clark had volunteered. He also didn't know that FDR had already called Gable himself and tried to talk him out of enlisting, but had received the same negative response.

Mayer was defeated. "Not only that," he told Strickling, "Roosevelt thanked us for the ten thousand dollars worth of war bonds."

"Five," Strickling corrected.

"He made it ten!" Mayer barked. "Actors! This is the only industry whose major assets walk out the door every night. And our biggest asset is about to get his ears shot off."

At this point I made the mistake that drew me into the most ludicrous plan of the war. Mannix happened to look out L.B.'s office window just at the moment that I was selling a signed 8x10 photo of Katharine Hepburn to one of the Washington Boulevard gate security guards. I don't know if it was the sale itself (Hepburn seldom gave autographs, and she certainly didn't in this particular case) or just because Mr. Strickling remembered me from the Gable house, but when Mannix asked him, "Who do we have here who's expendable?" my name came up.

Chapter 5

FIVE MINUTES LATER I was being escorted/led into Mr. Mayer's office at the end of what he detested calling the Thalberg Building. He hated Thalberg and competed with him, but ever since the "boy wonder"'s death in 1936 he had accepted him as part of the studio's legend. In any event, with Mr. Strickling's arm around my shoulder and him saying to me in an avuncular voice, "Call me Howard," we entered the Lion's den.

Unlike Harry Cohn at Columbia or Darryl Zanuck at Fox, Louis B. Mayer didn't need to have his desk on risers in order to assert himself over whoever sat in front of him. The man had charisma equal to one of his stars and, as I was shortly to learn, was every bit as talented an actor.

"Those are really something, aren't they?" Mr. Mayer said as he walked out to the anteroom to greet me. I was looking at his collection of Oscars®. I don't know what made me feel stranger: Louis B. Mayer coming to meet me, or my being there to meet him at all. "*Broadway Melody, Grand Hotel, Mutiny on the Bounty, The Great Ziegfeld, Gone with the Wind* — well, that one's on loan from Irene and David. The Academy is my idea, you know."

"Yes sir," I managed to agree. "You hosted a dinner in 1927 at the Ambassador Hotel where—." I didn't get to finish before Mr. Mayer said, "Very good, son. Howard said you knew your stuff."

"It's my job, sir."

"No, m'boy, it's more than a job. This has been your dream, hasn't it? It's a long way to MGM from 129 Franklin Avenue in Brooklyn."

How did he know this? Mr. Mannix hid my personnel folder behind his back.

"Some time I'd like to take you through the writers building. You know, we hire the best writers. John Lee Mahon, Samson Rafaelson, Don Stewart, um — Eddie, who was that broad?"

"Jane Murfin. She did *Pride and Prejudice*."

"I bet you'd love meeting those folks, wouldn't you?"

"Sure, Mr. Mayer," I said.

"Now, then , Alan," Mr. Mayer said, guiding me into his office, "I need your help. You may not believe this, but you're the only person in our whole Metro-Goldwyn-Mayer family that I can ask. Do you think you can find it in your heart to do Uncle Louis a favor?"

Now it was getting weird. Scary and weird.

"I would be in your debt, Alan. Very few people hold L.B. Mayer's marker."

I gulped. "What do you want me to do, Mr. Mayer?" By now he had guided me to his leather couch.

"I knew you'd say yes! We have a problem with Clark Gable. He's just done something very hot-headed. Do you know what he's done?"

I shook my head No.

"He's gone and enlisted in the Army Air Corps."

The words hung in the air. Mayer was waiting for my response. I knew it was a test. If I said, "But we need him at Metro" that would sound like sucking up. If I said, "That's great, what a patriot," it might sound like I chose America over MGM." In the end, all I could think of to say was, "I hear they're a good branch."

"Oh? You know about them?" Mayer asked.

"I tried to enlist, too."

Behind me, Mannix and Strickling exchanged doubting looks.

"No, really," I said. It happened to be true. When the Japanese bombed Pearl Harbor, like millions of other American men, I raced down to my local Army recruitment office and tried to enlist.

"Yes," Mayer continued, "and it broke your heart when they turned you down. You were classified 2-A, weren't you? Wasn't he, Eddie?"

Mannix opened my personnel folder. "Occupational deferment based on your employer's work for the U.S. Government," he read.

"That means you make training films," Mayer asked softly. "On your Army application, it said you make training films at Fort Roach. But you don't really make training films, do you?"

"No, Mr. Mayer." I think I blushed.

"In other words, m'boy, you lied to Uncle Sam."

"Honest, Uncle Louis, I wanted to get in the Army, but I thought I could get assigned to the Informational Unit because of my studio experience and all. You know the Army. They just naturally misunderstood. What I really want to do is direct."

"Nonsense," Mr. Mayer said, "you don't want to direct. You're coming along in publicity. What I want you to do is take charge of one special account. Can you guess what account? Don't bother, I'll tell you. Only the most important star we have here at the dream factory. The most important star in the world. Alan, I want you to take charge of Clark Gable."

I was, as Sam Goldwyn might say, both flabber and gasted. "You want me to handle The King?"

"That's right, m'boy," Mayer chuckled. "Side by side, you and Gable."

Foolishly, I said, "I don't know what to say, Mr. Mayer" and then, with equal foolishness, I shook his hand.

"You've just done Metro a great service," he pronounced, rising to his full short height. "You've done me a great service, too. Howard will take you right downtown."

"Downtown?"

"Of course," Uncle Louis said. "You can't handle Gable without joining the Army. That's where he enlisted, remember?"

"Whoa, did I miss something?" I protested.

Suddenly Uncle Louis was back to being Mr. Mayer. "Eddie, you talk to this kid."

"Look, kid," Mannix said, "Gable volunteered and his induction is next week. Then he's going to Miami for basic training. You take the train and meet him there. We'll tell the Army you got reassigned here at the studio and aren't making training films any more. That'll free you up to enlist. But here's the deal: We'll pull a few strings and get you assigned to the same unit at Clark. You stick with him, handle the press, and keep him out of trouble."

"What he means," Mayer said, becoming intense, "is that you keep him alive. He wants to go up in a plane? You nail him to the ground. He wants to pick up a gun? You take it away from him. You get him back here safe and sound. Got it?"

I must have stammered something incoherent because Mayer yelled, "What's your problem?"

"I want to serve my country," I managed, "not a movie star. I can't see how a phone call could make me fit for duty. I mean,

I'm glad it did, but I'd like to ponder this for a couple of days."

"Ponder all you want," Mannix broke in. "And while you're pondering that, ponder this." He started reading from my folder again. "Jenny LaRue and unidentified producer, September 3, 1941. Lucille Carney and unidentified producer, September 19. Frances DeShazo and unidentified producer, October 24 through 27, long weekend. We identified the producers. They've all had their parking spaces painted over. We're onto you, kid. You're a publicist, but you're also a sometimes-pimp for our producers and visiting theatre owners."

"Not only that," Strickling chimed in, "what about your black market in signed photos, costumes, and spying for the fan magazines?"

They had half of it wrong, but the other half was enough to nail me. Nevertheless, I bluffed, "I don't have to stand here and listen to this!"

"Yes you do," Mannix said, moving his bulky form toward me. "Look, in this town, any broad under thirty who ain't a starlet is a whore. We all know that. But you don't sign my name to the hotel bills and charge 'em to Metro. Forgery aside, it's called procurement and it gets you ten years. And if any of the broads was from out of state, you're lookin' at twenty years under the Mann Act. So what's it gonna be? Jail or Hitler?"

Strickling twisted the knife in my back. "Suddenly Alan Greenberg isn't so vital to the operation of the studio."

"On the contrary, Howard," said Mannix, by now thoroughly confusing the roles of good cop and bad cop. "Suddenly Alan Greenberg is absolutely vital to the operation of the studio." It was three on one. Mannix put his hand on my shoulder. "It's all settled, then. I'll have our travel office issue you a train ticket, then we'll go downtown for you to sign up, then you'll go home and pack a bag and lock up your little black book. You'll have a few days to get your affairs in order here, then you'll ride to Florida and hook up with Clark at the Collins Park training center in Miami."

"How does he feel about this?" I managed to ask.

"Ask him yourself," Strickling said, pushing me out Mayer's door and closing it behind me, saying, "he hates publicists and he doesn't know you're coming."

Chapter 6

WILLIAM CLARK GABLE RAISED his right hand to mirror the recruiting officer as the newsreel cameras rolled:

"You, Clark Gable, a citizen of the United States, do hereby voluntarily agree to enlist as a soldier in the United States Army; that you will support and defend the Constitution of the United States against all enemies, foreign and domestic; that you will bear true faith and allegiance to the same; and that you will obey the orders of the President of the United States and the orders of the officers appointed over you, according to regulations, the Uniform Code of Military Justice, and the articles of war, so help you God."

"I do."

Gable was not the only star to enlist in the war against fascism, but he was the biggest, and he made it a point to start at the bottom. By the time the hostilities ended, Hollywood had left its honorable mark. James Stewart flew air raids and achieved the rank of Brigadier General in the Air Force. Lee Marvin was a Private, First Class in the Marines. Charles Bronson was a tail gunner. Glenn Ford rose to the rank of Captain in the Navy. Charles Durning was a Ranger and emerged from the war as one of America's most decorated heroes. Mel Brooks was a photographer at the Battle of the Bulge. Frank Capra, John Huston, John Ford, George Stevens, William Wyler, and other directors made combat films. And there were countless others from all ranks of the motion picture industry, not all of them stars, but all of them patriots. Actresses such as Bette Davis, Marsha Hunt, Marlene Dietrich, and Veronica Lake joined less famous movie women in the Hollywood Canteen which was open every night to give servicemen a cup of coffee, a donut, a smile, and sometimes a dance with a screen legend.

Gable's enlistment was the best recruitment tool the Army could have asked for. Unfortunately, it came with a liability as big as the European theatre of war, as Clark discovered as soon as he said, "I do."

"Do you have a statement, Clark?" asked the first reporter. He was joined by a second who threw, "give us a statement, Private Gable" at him and a third who called out, "Over here, Private Gable." Clark was used to handling the press, and he stepped forward with the humor and aplomb that made him popular with audiences and reporters alike.

"Ladies and Gentlemen, there's nothing I've just done that hundreds of thousands of other Americans haven't already done to defend our country," he said calmly and carefully. "I've made application to be a gunner, and I'm going to do my very best."

"What're your dog tags gonna say, Private?" one of the men asked.

"Name, rank, and serial number," said the King with a smile. "That's all you'll get out of me, boys." Everyone laughed, then called out for "one more" photo of Clark and the recruiter, their hands raised in recreation of the swearing-in. As soon as it was over, Clark's next stop was Miami and basic training. That's where I was to join him.

I arrived at the Collins Park Hotel and Army Base on a muggy day. Even though it was still winter, Miami was steamy, and it was not to let up. Like many other civilian centers, the hotel had been commissioned for the war and transformed into a collision of peace-time elegance and military minimalism. The ballroom served as an assembly area and site of general confusion. Recruits bumped into each other, tripped over their duffel bags, and tried to read their assignments, like an anthill without a queen. From the looks on these kids' faces, most were away from home for the first time, It was also the first time for most of them meeting people who didn't look like themselves. Those of us from New York City were used to the varied palette of America, but I'd be willing to bet all my bar mitzvah pens that I was the first Jew that any of the guys from Iowa had ever set their guarded gaze upon. The services were still racially segregated at the time and, to make it worse, the South was infected with Jim Crow, so the recruits of color had it doubly hard. All I had to tolerate was the odd sense that people were checking out my haircut until it hit me that what they were looking for was horns. (Later I told them that we Jews only wear those on high holidays.)

Somehow I found my way to the makeshift barracks that had once been luxury rooms and suites. No more. Walls had been knocked out, plush mattresses had been replaced with cots, and there were no more doors for privacy. There I met the proverbial bomber crew assortment of fellow recruits with whom I was to experience basic training. Where they had been sent here by the luck of the draw, I had been deposited in their midst by the pull of Metro. If Louis B. Mayer couldn't keep Clark Gable out of the U.S. Army, then he could damn well sew me to Gable's side as his guardian angel.

The beds were lined up in two rows facing each other. Each was narrow and single; no bunk beds here. The kids — for that's what we all were —in our group were all between 18 and 21 and were trying to act older and tougher. A rough-looking, rusty-haired Polish kid named Lewko was giving attitude to a dark-haired Italian guy, Battista, whom I later learned was Cuban. Molina, an actual Italian with dark features, and Jeffers, slight and pale and Michigan corn-fed, were playing poker on a green Army blanket stretched regulation-taut over a bunk that was empty except for a duffel bag resting at its foot. The beds on either side were still empty, which I thought unusual, so I took one, innocently asking, "Either of these taken?"

Battista motioned "be my guest," so I piled my bag onto it. The others grinned at me in some kind of privately shared joke.

"What, did somebody drop a turd?" I asked.

"Yeah, he's in the bunk next to yours," Lewko cracked. When I looked vague, Lewko put his hands behind his ears to make them stick out. "Rhett Butler slept here," he said. I reached down and looked at the name tag on the duffel bag at the foot of the turd's bed. It had "C. Gable" stenciled on it.

"Is that really him?" I faked disbelief.

Molina groused, "Sure looked like him. Taller than he looks on screen. And he pretended to be friendly"

"Pretended?" I asked. I was still trying to find out more. "Clark is—I mean, I hear that Gable is one of the nicest guys around."

"Fuckin' asshole movie star," grunted Battista.

"And who the fuck are you?" Lewko asked, standing in front of me.

"Name's Alan Greenberg."

"Oh, a Hebrew, huh?" he said.

"We prefer to call ourselves Christ-killers," I smiled. When it occurred to me that sarcasm wasn't Lewko's strong suit, I changed to, "Jew is fine. But I'll answer to Alan. Who are you?"

They all introduced themselves, but Lewko remained standoffish.

"I was kidding about killing Christ," I said. "I'm from New York. We have a pretty rough sense of humor there."

"Jesus was never in New York," Lewko said. "Where did you kill him?"

"Actually," I said, trying one more time for the sake of the others, and, let's face it, grandstanding for myself. "The Jews didn't do it. It was a hit by one of the New Jersey families." Crickets. "You can read about it in the Gospel of St. Lucky of Luciano. Can we do this some other time?

"Are all New Yorkers assholes?" Molina asked.

"Some of us are worse," I said. "I've been living in Los Angeles so long, a lot of New York has worn off. You'll understand after a while."

"I'm not sure I want to. Stay away from me or I'll show you how we still take care of people back east."

Jeffers perked up at hearing about Los Angeles. "Do you know any movie stars?" he asked fawningly.

"You have no idea," I said drolly.

"I saw Alice Fay once in a motorcade through Detroit," he said proudly. "I think she waved at me."

"I hear they're all over the place in Hollywood," said Lewko.

"Hollywood is a factory town," I said, "like Detroit or Chicago. The difference is, instead of cars or pork bellies, we make movies."

"Like that fuckin' asshole movie star," Battista repeated.

"Right," I scowled. "So, uh, where is the, uh, fuckin' asshole movie star now?"

"Gettin' his fuckin' hair cut," said Battista.

"Where would that be?" I asked.

"At the fuckin' barber shop," Battista said, like it was my fault.

"You won't get lost. Just follow the fuckin' cameras."

Oh God, the press was here already. "Okay," I said, racing from the hall. "Fuckin' thanks."

Battista was right. It wasn't hard to follow the cameras. The tough part was pushing through them to take charge without looking like what I was doing, which was a publicist taking charge. The barber shop, set up to shear recruits like sheep, had been cleared for the occasion. Gable sat in the chair, a smock covering his fatigues, with the military barber giving what must have been the slowest, most attentive haircut since he, himself, had been drafted.

"Well, Clark, how do you feel about losing the most famous moustache in movies?" one reporter asked.

Joked Gable, "Frankly, my dear, I don't give a damn."

"What about talk of the studio trying to keep you stateside like some of other actors?" another asked.

"I'm not here to dump on other guys," Gable said without making it sound like a rebuke. "I'm here to dump on Hitler." Then he turned to the barber. "All right, Bernardo, do your duty."

As Bernardo started to really go to work, so did I. I jumped in front of the cameras and held up my hands. "No pictures. C'mon boys, no more pictures." I was greeted by an angry chorus of "What's the big idea?" and "Hey, buddy, down in front."

Gable was more irritated at me than he was at them. "What's the big idea?" he said. "I'm through with being handled like I'm some precious flower. Let 'em get their pictures and they'll go away."

"I'm with the studio," I said.

Gable looked at me sharply, then made that, "oh, no, I shoulda figured" grimace that made him famous, and shot back, "Well, I'm not."

"Please, sir, I'm just here to run interference. Pay no attention."

"I'm not planning to, and I'm not sir, I'm a private."

I had to think fast. I told the photographers, "Mr. Gable will pose for exclusive pictures as soon as he's finished here. Until then, I'll have to ask you to leave the room so the barber can do his job."

"What about our job?" one of the cameramen said.

Gable stared at me. Something in him clicked.

"I'll explain," I said out of the side of my mouth.

"You'd better," he said out of the side of his. Then he smiled at the press. "Okay, boys, this won't take long. When we're through I'll give each of you five minutes alone." With that, they grumbled but left to wait outside. Bernardo the barber didn't move.

"Who the hell are you?" Gable asked me.

"Alan Greenberg."

"Who sent you?"

"Howard Strickling. And Mr. Mayer."

"Protecting their investment, eh?" he said, running through a selection of facial expressions. I ignored them all.

"Protecting you," I said firmly.

"I can take care of myself."

"Oh yeah?" I heard myself say. "Those photographers, did you see where they were standing?"

"What's your point?"

"They were all gonna shoot you head-on. You know what that means, don't you?"

Gable seemed chastened. I couldn't believe it. "When I'm photographed from the front," he repeated as if it had been drilled into him, which it had been, "my ears stick out like a taxi cab with the doors open." He gave it some thought. "Okay, Greenberg, you made your point. Just don't order these guys around, see? They gotta earn a living."

Immediately I realized that I had just been chewed out by the biggest movie star in the world. Only I didn't feel chewed out, I felt like I wanted this man as my best friend. That's why he was popular with both men and women everywhere. Without even trying, he was the Real Thing.

"I understand, Mr. Gable," I finally said in a more conversational tone.

He offered me his hand. "Private Gable." We shook.

"Private Greenberg," I added.

"What outfit you with?"

"Um, yours."

"Where are you bunked?" he asked suspiciously.

"Next to you."

Gable rolled his eyes. It was another of his famous expressions that, without question, meant, "You wanna bet?"

"I don't need a publicist," he said. "This is not a movie. I am not the star."

I pointed out the barber shop window to the reporters gathered to interview him and the cameramen waiting to take his picture. "Tell them. Tell the public. People everywhere want to know everything about your enlistment, Private Gable. You're the best recruiting poster there is. You've got to know that."

"No way," Gable said. "I will not be known as the only private in the United States Army with his own orderly."

"How do you think the orderly feels about it?" I said in frustration.

"Since we agree," he said, "one of us should transfer. I volunteer you."

Before I could answer, I saw the barber stooping on the floor. He was gathering Gable's cut hair into a paper bag. "What are you doing?" I asked Bernardo.

"What does it look like," he said without looking up.

"Like you're gonna sell locks of Private Gable's hair."

"That's what I'm doing."

Gable's hearty laugh put me in my defensive place. "Bernardo," he said, "you could run a movie studio." He stepped from the chair, threw off his smock, slapped Bernardo on the back, and joined the photographers waiting outside the room. I started to leave, but Bernardo put one hand on my shoulder. He held shears in the other. "Just a minute," he said. "Where are you going? You need a haircut, private."

Bernardo finished long before the photographers did, and I joined Clark as he graciously dismissed them. "That's how it's done," he said. "Otto said to always respect them and they'll respect you, but don't ever let 'em go too far." He looked at my haircut. "You need to keep your hair longer when this war is over."

"Sorry about Otto," I said. "He was a good publicist."

"He was a friend. Most publicists are like remora around sharks. Best to let them do their job and don't pay attention. And you can always bite them if you need to. No offense."

"None taken," I lied. "I guess it's different where you are. Most actors on the way up would kill to be recognized. Then they go out in public wearing sunglasses so nobody will know who they are."

"You're talking about other guys," Gable said, staring ahead. "Do you know, I've had my phone number listed ever since I moved out here."

"Don't you get a lot of phone calls?"

"Never." He smiled at me. "Who'd ever think that *that* Clark Gable would be in the phone book?" As we walked, two G.I.s headed toward us. "Look straight ahead," Gable said in a stage whisper. "Just do it." As the men passed, one whispered loud enough for us to hear, "They must be making a movie."

"The only press agent I ever trusted was Otto Winkler," Gable said, "and he died with Carole. I don't need another one."

"I'm sorry for your grief," I repeated. "I truly am. But the Army wants you for the war effort and my job is to make you look good."

"If I wanted to look good," he said, "I never woulda filmed *Parnell.*"

I started to laugh but from behind us a loud voice shouted, "Ten-HUT!" We both snapped to attention as a drill sergeant circled around and got in Clark's face. His name tag said "Sgt. Daly" and it was stuck on a chest that looked as solid as the anger glowing in his tiny eyes. I didn't know then, and I don't know now, who in his right mind would want to be a drill sergeant, but whatever it took, Daly was a good one. The problem was that he was not a good man.

"Just because you're famous, don't think you're gonna get special treatment," he spit at the King. "You're just another dumb-ass green recruit like all these other scumbags. Don't you ever forget it."

"Yes, Sergeant," Gable answered clearly.

"So don't go lookin' for favors," Daly kept going. "Your movie star ass ain't no different from anybody else's, and I don't care what some faggot tells me. You got it?"

"Yes, Sergeant," Gable said. "Can I ask a question?"

"Go ahead."

"I know I'm no different than anyone else. But would you mind telling that to the other men?"

Sergeant Daly's face searched for a clue whether Gable was being wise or a wise-ass. Not figuring it out, he said, "I got your number, movie star. I'm gonna make you my career." Then, seeing that he had left me out, he bent into my face and said, "And you, you little yid, you're gonna be my hobby." Standing again, he barked, "Dismissed!" and we moved on.

"Are you sure you want this gig?" I asked Gable.

He responded, "Are you sure you don't?"

Chapter 7

I DON'T CARE HOW immune you think you can get to seeing movie stars in person, when Clark Gable kicks you in the ass at 5 A.M. to wake up, nothing will ever be the same again.

'Up and at 'em, Junior," Gable said as he planted his combat boot in my rear. I would have rolled over and pulled my Army blanket over my head but I knew the next kick would be in my groin.

"What time is it?" I said as reveille died out in the distance.

"Five A.M.," Gable said and yanked on the blanket, dumping me onto the barracks floor. "Seventeen years of six A.M. studio calls, twelve hour days, six and a half days a week taught me how to wake up at five and be civil."

"You don't have to be so Goddamned cheerful about it," I muttered.

"See you at mess, Junior," he said, and left for breakfast while the others stretched, coughed, and scratched themselves for the first day of basic. Two minutes later my beloved Sergeant Daly stormed in and scared all of us awake, into the showers, and out of there in five minutes flat.

BY WIRE TO HOWARD STRICKLING VICE
PRESIDENT PUBLICITY MGM STUDIOS
CULVER CITY CALIFORNIA STOP KING
PROGRESSING WELL BASIC TRAINING STOP
ON FAST TRACK TO OFFICERS CANDIDATE
SCHOOL STOP OTHER RECRUITSD TAKING
HIM INTO THEIR HEARTS STOP GREENBERG

I was lying my ass off in my first cable to Metro. For starters, when Clark sat down with his tray to join the other guys in the mess hall, all of them acted like he was invisible. I sat across from him, but this time he acted as if I were invisible.

"Gee, this food sure isn't like the studio commissary," I said, trying to start a conversation.

Silence.

"In fact, it isn't like any other kind of food I've ever tasted." Second try. Gable looked as if his mind was three thousand miles away. If he was hurt by the others, he hid it. He just shoveled in his food as fast as he could, bused his tray, and walked out into the Florida sunrise.

"Fuckin' asshole movie star," Battista said. "Wouldn't say hello or anything."

KING CENTER OF ATTENTION AT MEALS
STOP FINDS ARMY CHOW A COMEDOWN
FROM STUDIO COMISSARY STOP WE BOTH
MISS MR MAYER'S MATZO BALL SOUP STOP
GREENBERG

I guess I stared too long at the other guys because Lewko stared back at me with a layer of challenge. I wondered what they were all thinking. Was it because Gable was famous or because they thought he was trying too hard to fit in. Nah. These guys didn't have a clue what twenty years of unremitting fame can do to somebody, even somebody as grounded as everybody says Gable was.

Case in point. Before I got to know him, I was at an exhibitors meeting where we trotted out the stars for visiting theatre owners and tried to inspire them to meet our contract terms (which were stiffer than other studios). All these guys are standing around bitching about having to pay seventy percent of the gate instead of sixty percent, and Gable walks in. Nobody ahead of him, nobody with him, he just walks into the room. The place goes dead quiet. He's got to know that they're all looking at him, gawking even. He goes up to the nearest man and shakes his hand. "Clark Gable," he says. Turns to the next guy. "Clark Gable. How do you do?" And he keeps going like that. He was the only person in the room who didn't have to introduce himself, but that's exactly what he did. Talk about being one of the guys.

All except these guys, apparently. But it's got to change. I guess it's the duty of basic training to make us hate the enemy more than we hate each other.

Going through drills and exercises, I underestimated Gable. Here's a 41-year-old guy drilling with a company of 18-to-22-year olds. I'm 23 and even I had a tough time keeping up. How does he do it? He must be right about the rigors of filmmaking keeping him in shape. And between pictures when he didn't have to be on the set and ready to go by 6 A.M., there were his legendary hunting, fishing, and outdoor activities. He's even giving the drill sergeant, who's got to be as old as him, a run. Why the guy has to pick on Gable is anybody's guess. Jealousy? Insecurity? Or just being a prick? Last week Gable was keeping up with everybody else on a five-mile forced march, full load of gear, and Sergeant Daly started pacing alongside him shouting insults. Here was Gable, setting the pace for the whole company, and this moron tries to mess it up. And when he still couldn't trip him up verbally, he stuck his booted foot out and tripped me.

TO HOWARD STRICKLING STOP THEY SAY THIS IS THE HOTTEST MIAMI AUGUST ON RECORD BUT THAT HASN'T KEPT ARMY FROM GIVING REAL WORKOUT STOP KING IN TOP SHAPE STOP HAS FORMED SOLID RELATIONSHIP WITH DRILL SERGEANT WHO RESPECTS HIM AND TREATS HIM SAME AS EVERYBODY ELSE STOP GREENBERG

What else can I tell them? That they should call the White House and have Sergeant Daly assigned to the Gestapo where he'd feel more at home? There's a difference between being a hardass and being an asshole. Perhaps he thinks it's like your first day at school where, if you spot a potential bully, the best thing to do is go and punch the guy in the kisser before he has a chance to start picking on you, and that settles it. Of course, that makes you the bully. But power-mad martinets like Daly never consider that. Only guys like me who get picked on.

At any rate, I didn't put any of that in the cables I sent Metro. In fact, I didn't even dare use the name Gable. Never mind keeping military secrets from the enemy. I had to keep them from the fan magazines. They'd love to get their hands on anything they could sell papers with, like one afternoon on the rifle range.

TO STRICKLING STOP KING EXCELLENT
MARKSMAN STOP PRACTICES ON OWN TIME
STOP CREDITS YEARS OF SKEET SHOOTING,
HUNTING, AND SPECIAL LOVE FOR MR.
MAYER STOP GREENBERG.

This time I told the truth in my cable to the studio. Gable was indeed a terrific shot. What I didn't tell them, of course, was that, instead of a normal target, Gable had managed to get photos of Mr. Mayer to tack up in the bulls-eye spot—and he hardly ever missed.

But the men still avoided him even as he tried to pull them into whatever he did. The result was a sad tug-of-war that started to erode what little company morale was just starting to develop. For example, after a fiendish workout during the day, the guys decided to burn a little of their sleeping time playing poker. Lewko, Molina, Jeffers, and Battista found a deck of relatively unmarked cards and were intensely into the game. Most of the other soldiers were writing home, shaving, reading, or rubbing liniment on whatever they could reach that was sore. I was writing a letter home when I saw Jeffers look up from his cards and snatch glances at Gable. Gable ignored him — in fact, he had perfected the ability to ignore everything — but after a while it was obvious that Jeffers was searching his brain for some excuse to come over and simply say hello. To do this, however, meant that he would have to brave the harassment of Lewko, Molina, and Battista. Was I right about saying this was like high school? Gable sat quietly spit-polishing his shoes, completely indifferent to the studied indifference around him. I composed in my head the report I'd send to the studio in the morning:

KING ALWAYS INCLUDED BARRACKS
ACTIVITIES STOP PEOPLE AMAZED SOMEONE
SO FAMOUS COULD FIT IN SO WELL STOP
GREENBERG

It stuck in my brain. It wasn't just a lie, it was a fantasy. Something came over me. I was trying to protect a man who had spent his career, if not his life, protecting himself against people who said they were trying to protect him but actually wanted something from him. Gable didn't need protecting. He needed company. No he didn't. He needed Lombard.

It was while we were pulling latrine patrol courtesy of Sergeant Daly (no special reason) that I tried to offer an olive branch. Watching the King of Hollywood scrub and polish a row of urinals, I thought how humble he looked. Then I thought how damaging it would be if somebody happened to sneak a picture, and, in a fit of paranoia, I stood up, ran to the bubble glass window high up the bathroom wall, and then ran over to the door to make sure both were closed. When I finished, I saw that Gable was watching me.

"What on earth are you up to, Junior?" he asked.

I outlined the risk of being caught doing this duty, and tried joking, "Are you sure Mr. Mayer started like this?" It was all I could think of. Gable went back to his job. "Flush twice," I said, "it's a long way to the studio."

This time Gable threw the wet brush on the floor. It was as close as I'd seen him come to losing his temper. "You don't have to give them a hard time just because I do."

I felt ashamed. "Sorry."

"I'm not here to do MGM a favor or make your life easier. I'm here to fight a war. The sooner other people realize that, the sooner I'll be able to get down to business."

Before I could say anything, the latrine door flew open and the drill sergeant presented himself. We stood. "At ease," he said. Then he started inspecting our work.

"If the fan magazines could see you now!" He began circling Gable. "The King on his knees cleaning up other people's piss." Then he turned his sights on me. "And a Jewboy cleaning up after the King."

He gloated at my obvious desire to push my bristle brush into his face. I weighed the pleasure versus the punishment and remembered that I was here to look after Clark, not defend the tribe of Abraham. Sergeant Daly read my mind. "Were you about to say something in Hebrew?"

Gable plopped his brush into his pail with a deliberateness calculated to make the drill sergeant wonder, if only for a moment, whether he was finished cleaning or preparing to explode. The two men stared at each other and I swear I saw the drill sergeant blink.

"Just to show you how pleased I am with the fine job you two have done here in my little powder room," said the bully with the sergeant stripes, "I think I'll reward you with a trip to the beach."

It was nine P.M. and reveille was coming along in eight hours. Gable and I looked at each other. This could not be good.

Chapter 8

WHEN I WAS A teenager in Brooklyn the code word for asking a girl to spend time alone with you was inviting her down to Jamaica Bay to watch the submarine races. Little did I know that, after December 7, 1941, there was a very real fear along both coasts of the United States that there really would be submarines poised off shore ready to attack. There were a few jokes made that if submarines ever dared to chug up New York's East River they would dissolve in the pollution. But in Miami, Florida, in the summer of 1942, the fear of German U-Boats was real enough that the government built watch towers along the coast and ordered guys like Gable and me to staff them.

It was Sergeant Daly's idea, however, to have us do it in full battle dress starting on a ninety-degree afternoon "just in case." He said it with the sneer that came easily to him. "You have to be the first to do battle with the Axis on American land," he said.

Typical of the Army, we had only one pair of binoculars between us. The tower stood like a glorified lifeguard station, and by the time we trudged through the sand and pulled our way to the tree-fort-sized enclosure we were exhausted. A storm was brewing and, with our luck, would probably start pounding us just as we were being relieved and had to walk back to the barracks.

Even with the sun setting in the west behind us, the chance of catching rays reflecting off a conning tower were slim. After an hour of this, I asked Gable, "See any U-Boats yet?"

"No, and I don't expect to see them any more than the Sergeant does," he said. "Remember last February somebody thought they saw a Jap sub off Santa Barbara and all hell broke loose? They called it the battle of Hollywood."

"Yeah," I said. "How can people be so gullible?"

"Why don't you tell me? You're a publicist."

That was unnecessary, I thought, and decided, King or not, I'd had enough. "Why don't you stop riding that horse?"

"Admit it," Gable said, digging, "your job is to con the price of a ticket out of people and make up hooey about guys like me."

"Oh, we do other things, too," I said, seeing how far I could go. "One of our busiest jobs is keeping people's drug habits, paternity suits, abortions, hit-and-runs, and other 'hooey' out of the papers. Did you hear about the director driving home from an all-night party who ran over a kid on a bicycle in the Palisades delivering newspapers?"

"No," Gable said.

"Did you hear about the leading lady who decided to take a long vacation in Ohio where she had her married leading man's baby scraped out of her?"

Gable raised his binoculars and scanned the ocean. "I see your point."

I was steamed. "I know you don't like me 'cause I'm a publicist. Or maybe you just don't like me, period. I don't care. But there's a bigger war to fight, so how about we call a truce between us and take on Hitler?"

I thought I'd made my point. I was breathing hard. I felt tense.

Gable lowered his binoculars and stared into my eyes the way he took on Captain Bligh in *Mutiny on the Bounty*. Then he laughed that Gable laugh. "That is some of the worst dialogue I've ever heard, including in my own pictures."

I cracked a smile and laughed along with him. He also relaxed and, for the first time, seemed to see past my job and into me as a person.

"Look, Junior," he said, "I'm lucky and I know it. It's just, the hard thing about bein' Clark Gable is that everybody expects you to be Clark Gable. The only one who never fell for that malarkey was Ma."

"Your mother?"

"Carole."

Gable's eyes drifted and I realized too late that I had opened up a King-sized can of worms.

"I called her Ma and she called me Pa. We met at a party, some movie thing. We weren't free at the time, but that didn't stop her. She called me, can you believe it? At first we hung out, then one thing led to another and the romance was on. She could swear better'n the guys, but she was all woman, and she knew what the words meant. God, people loved her. Remember a show called *My Man Godfrey?* She and William Powell has been married and then got divorced, but the minute Bill read the script, he knew Carole would be perfect for it. He asked for her as his co-star. Can you believe it? What can you say about a girl that even her ex-husband still likes her?"

He turned away from me and talked into the approaching storm clouds. "I'm the one who sent her on that bond drive, you know. I'm the reason she took a plane home. It shoulda been me."

A bolt of lightning cracked. It hit the tower and the wood burst into flame.

"Jesus Christ!" I screamed. Gable didn't flinch. He stood there, just stood there. I grabbed his shirt and pulled him to the ladder, but he didn't move. He shrugged me off and just stood there like a statue.

"Come on, let's go!"

"Save yourself, Junior."

"F'r'Chrissake, you don't want to die in basic training, do you? The ladder's right here." The glow of the fire showed me the stoic look on his face. This was stupid. It wasn't even enemy fire, it was fire-fire.

"CLARK!" I'd never called him Clark before. "Clark, move your goddamn ass."

He snapped back to reality. "You go first, Junior," he said calmly. The fire caught onto the roof. We only had seconds before everything collapsed on us.

"Not with your death wish, I won't," I said.

"You go first!"

"No, you."

"Don't give me Alphonse and Gaston," he said, "get out now," and pushed me from of the tower onto the sand and tossed my gear on top of me. Then he casually climbed down the ladder to safety.

In the distance we could hear the fire brigade working its way toward us. I tugged at Gable's shoulder to get him to follow me, but he sluffed me off.

"Come on, we gotta go. The fire brigade'll here, then the reporters. You know that."

But Gable didn't move. He was staring at the fire. No, he was staring through the fire. I took a chance and said into his ear, "You didn't make the plane crash, Clark. Do you understand that? It's not your fault. Clark? Clark?"

I know he heard me. He turned and followed me back to the barracks, saying nothing. But I knew he heard me.

Chapter 9

HENRY HARLEY ARNOLD WAS a different kind of general. While Eisenhower, Patton, Bradley, Clark, and Marshall were known for their battlefield and command brilliance, Arnold — nicknamed "Hap" — was the brains of the American effort to defeat the Axis. A General of both the U. S. Army and the U.S. Army Air Corps (which was created on his watch), he also helped form the government's wartime Project RAND which became the influential RAND Corporation think tank after the war.

Under Arnold, a small division of flyers in the U.S. Army became the Army Air Corps in 1942. His rise to command position was neither fast nor easy; prodigies are seldom appreciated by bureaucrats, and Hap — he supposedly received the nickname because of his upbeat disposition — endured more than his share of internecine struggle. But by the summer of 1942 he had been handed the controls by executive order of President Roosevelt himself, and began building the aerial arsenal of democracy.

One of his most public activities was pinning lieutenant's bars on Private Clark Gable, skipping the intermediate ranks and making him the poster child for recruitment. And "poster child" is the correct term, since that's what was expected of Clark as he endured the promotion ceremony in front of the newsreel cameras. "Miami Beach," the announcer intoned as the film unspooled in hundreds of theatres across the nation, "former vacationland for northern snowbirds, now where the Army Air Corps makes men out of boys, and officers out of men."

If the narration sounded more purple than usual for a newsreel, it was because the sight of General Arnold and Lieutenant Gable saluting and shaking hands inspired it. Clark was already a role model for men, and now he was being served up as an inspiration to boys — enlistment-age boys, that is. And just to show that you didn't have to be a movie star to get ahead in the service, once the narration ended, Arnold proclaimed, "And so it is my duty, and my honor, to confirm your commission as officers in the United States Army Air Corps."

"Officers" was indeed plural, for I was also promoted to Lieutenant (thank you, Mr. Mayer), not because I earned the rank, but because I needed it in order to continue my secondary assignment to cover the King. You can tell from looking at the footage that none of the other men present at the ceremony was particularly eager to be standing in Gable's shadow. The group of us that had gone through basic together — Lewko, Battista, Molina and Jeffers — seemed fated to remain as a unit, if not a retinue. They had come to accept Clark in the way that one tolerates an in-law: you can't get rid of him, so you might as well be polite, but don't cross any lines. God knows what they said in their letters to their families back home, or if they even wrote any. Even after fourteen weeks of hell Clark still had not broken through with them, and it didn't help when he was singled out to address the troops. After Arnold spoke, Clark stepped to the podium and unfolded a paper, pretending to read from it, but to me it was obvious that he had already memorized it in order to appear spontaneous before the cameras.

"Men," he began, "I've worked with you, scrubbed with you, marched with you, cursed with you — and, finally, this day is here. The important thing — the proud thing I've learned about us — is that we're fighters. We are Americans. Soon we'll wear officers' uniforms. How we look in 'em isn't important, it's how we wear them. Our job is to stay on the beam until, in victory, we get the command to Fall Out!"

The crowd cheered and Arnold hustled Clark off the platform. I pushed through the assemblage to try to follow them. At first I was blocked by the sheer number, but suddenly a hand reached out and yanked me through. You can just barely see me in the corner of the newsreel as the announcer wraps up the story saying, "After the ceremony, Lieutenant Gable personally asked General Arnold for assignment to gunnery school. After years of shooting movies, the King wants to shoot back — at Hitler."

Inside General Arnold's office, the mood was far less glib. Both Clark and I stood at rigid attention while "Hap" was anything but happy.

"Are you out of your mind?" he began without even any pleasantries.

"Permission to speak freely, sir," Gable asked.

"No!" Arnold commanded, and gave Gable the same intense stare that Gable had so often given his screen villains. Then he melted, "All right, out with it. At ease."

"What am I here for, General, if it's not to fight?"

Rather than answer directly, Arnold lifted a handful of scripts off his desk and tossed them at me. Unready for it, I missed and they scattered over the floor. So did I.

"It's my job," Arnold began, "to turn out training films that'll teach city boys what a Jeep is and farm boys what a toilet is. Some of the films sound pretty stupid, but they could save lives: 'How to Purify Water,' 'You Gas Mask and You,' 'How to Fold Your Parachute,' 'Don't Tuck in Your T-Shirt Like the Germans Do,' 'How to Keep From Getting the Clap' —"

"Who plays the title role in that one?" I asked, taking "at ease" too far.

"We wanted Donald Duck," Arnold said, and he wasn't kidding, "but Disney said that'd be like if MGM gave us Clark Gable." He let the words sink in with Gable, who got the picture. Then Arnold softened.

"Don't worry, Lieutenant, we're talking to Private SNAFU's agent about that one. You see, most people think movies are just for fun. But they can also be propaganda — the good kind, not the kind Dr. Goebbels makes. I can't begin to tell you how many fights I've had with Congress over that. They see the need to mold public opinion and build morale, but they don't see that movies and radio are the best way to do it. Someday they will, but if we don't start doing it now, that someday might be in German." He sat on the edge of his desk and spoke with Gable as if the two of them were doing an Andy Hardy film between Mickey Rooney and Lewis Stone. "I can't order you to do this for us, Clark, but I would like you to volunteer."

"Meaning no disrespect, General, but I came here to fight."

Arnold flawlessly switched gears. "Up in a plane, Clark, you're just one more guy with one more gun and one life to lose. If you die, your only legacy will be a headline. But as Clark Gable of the First Motion Picture Unit, you can lead a recruiting drive that'll fill the ranks with —"

Gable gave Arnold one of his "says you" stares, but the General was ready for him and returned fire with the biggest gun he had.

"Your late wife knew the importance of symbolism, of getting out there in person to sway others. Don't you want to continue the work she started?"

"I know what you want me to do, General," Clark started. "All my life I've been handed things. This acting business, I got lucky, is all. There's a hundred guys more talented than me, and their ears don't stick out, but I'm the one that got the job. With this war, I want to finally do something I can be proud of."

Once more Arnold changed his tactic. I could see him do it. He was that good. He had the power to order Gable to do whatever was required and Gable knew it. So why were they behaving like this was a negotiation? But Arnold knew that there are two ways to get someone to do something: order them, or inspire them to do it on their own. With Clark, Arnold wanted the latter, and it was starting to work.

"You know the worst job in the entire Air Corps? I'll show you." He stood up and led us to the next room. "You too, Greenbaum."

"Greenberg"

"Whatever."

Inside Arnold's conference room the walls were pasted with stills, drawings, and production boards for movies just like we had at Metro. But there was also a model of a B-17 hanging from the ceiling with one side cut away so you could see its interior. I'd marveled at miniatures like this made by the studio's expert craftsmen, and this stood — rather, hung — with the best of them.

"This is the B-17-G Flying Fortress," Arnold said. "It's as big as — well, let's just say it's a hell of a target up there." He pointed the details as he described them. "Crew of ten: Pilot, co-pilot, flight engineer who doubles as top turret gunner, bombardier, navigator, who also doubles on turret, radio operator with an auxiliary turret, two waist gunners port and starboard, tail gunner, and ball turret gunner. Ball turret is mainly what we need recruits for. You get a clear view in all directions and no protection in any of 'em. You know the mortality rate for ball turret gunners?" Gable didn't know and shook his head. Said Arnold, "You don't want to."

"Even if I volunteer?" Gable asked.

"Denied," Arnold said emphatically. "First, you're too tall. They call it a ball turret because your knees bend up so far you kiss your balls. Second, or maybe it's first, you think the hell I want Clark Gable killed on my watch?"

"Then what am I here for, sir?"

The general ignored him. "We're calling the film *Combat America.* You'll train here, then go to England next spring with the 351st Bombardment Group."

Gable was surprised. "Next spring? The war could be over by then."

"Then you'll help build the peace. Meanwhile, nobody in this unit gets shipped to any front unless he knows what he's doing. Anyway, face it," Arnold said, softening, "at your age you're never gonna fly. You might qualify as wing gunner but there's no way you're getting in the cockpit even if you weren't Clark Gable. I'm sorry, but that's regulations."

"Jimmy Stewart's in his middle thirties, General," Clark tried. "That's no spring chicken."

"There's a lot of years between 34, which I happen to know Captain Stewart is, and 41, which I happen to know you are. Anyway, Stewart flopped his physical twice for being underweight, and he only got in as an instructor. C'mon, Gable, don't make this any harder for either of us. Take the assignment. By the time you're transferred to England you'll be promoted to Captain, have your own special living quarters, eat in the Combat Officers Mess, have special leave privileges —"

Gable shook his head. "If it's all the same to you and the Army, General, I'll stick with the other guys. If I've gotta depend on 'em for my life, we better get to know each other."

"That's the spirit," Arnold said, finally able to agree with what he'd wanted to hear all along. "Stay with your men. That's leadership."

"*Combat America*, huh?" Gable seemed intrigued. "I suppose I can make one picture if it'll get me closer to the action."

"There you go," Arnold smiled, putting his hand on my shoulder. I stood back at attention. "You and your assistant will ship out together."

Clark looked at me in horror. "My assistant?"

I returned his gaze with a grin I once saw in a Tom and Jerry cartoon. Without knowing it, General Arnold had placed Gable right where Louis B. Mayer wanted him.

Chapter 10

SUMMER OF 1942 TO the spring of 1943 was a harrowing time for America. War rationing, designed to boost unanimity, cut into the nation's food, driving, recreation, and building habits. Women replaced men in the workplace, and Rosie the Riveter became an enduring symbol of the ability of women to do anything a man could do short of earning the same salary. It was a consciousness that would remain after the war and blossom many years later, but that's another story.

At the beginning of 1943, Allied victory was nowhere near being a certainty. In early 1942, Japanese advances in Burma, Singapore, Malaya, and other Asian countries seemed invincible. Germany barely held its own against Russian forces with both sides sustaining unimaginable losses. At the same time, the Allies were still squabbling over long-term strategy with America urging a full-scale assault on Germany itself while the British proposed encircling the Nazis with numerous fronts. By the end of the year, however, Allied forces had scored victories against Hitler in Northern Africa and the Russians stopped the Germans at Stalingrad. The turning point was at Midway when the Pacific fleet rousted the Japanese. More than two years of grueling fighting lay ahead, but no one could know that. Even so, with every notice of triumph, Gable fell further into depression that it would be over before he could play his part.

I don't think he wanted to kill. But I worried that he wanted to die.

Victory was far from in the cards when our unit shipped off to England at the beginning of 1943. Lewko, Battista, Molina, and Jeffers had coalesced into a crackerjack filmmaking unit capable of handling both the bulky 16mm Mitchell cameras that we used for studio and solid set-up where sound recording was required, and the far more versatile hand-held Bell and Howell combat cameras which were used to shoot silent footage. Lewko and Molina were usually on camera; Battista on sound; and Jeffers keeping track of continuity. I kept track of Gable, and Gable, when he wasn't in front of the camera or being loaned to another unit, told us what we could do with our equipment. Everyone was professional, but no more.

Nothing had changed when we shipped off for England in March of 1943. Optimists called it a hop across the pond, but when you're on a troop ship with your fingers and toes fused into good luck crosses against being torpedoed by a German U-Boat, it's not as much a hop as it is frantically treading the emotional water until you land in England. Up till this time, the only things British I had seen were Greer Garson when she was being herself and Norma Shearer when she was being pretentious. No sooner had we arrived in Blighty than Clark and I were driven (on the wrong side of the road, which is a nerve-wracking experience the first couple of times you do it; you keep grabbing for a steering wheel that isn't there) to Polebrook.

The main Limey complaint about us Yanks at this time was "overpaid, oversexed, and over here," a not-so-subtle stab at our superior economy, our un-British bedroom attitudes, and George M. Cohan.

It was easy to counter by saying that the Brits were full of themselves and obnoxiously English until we were taken through whole villages that had been devastated by the Blitz or starved to abandonment by wartime shortages. Indeed, had it not been for the legendary British resolve and unswerving unanimity, plus the leadership of Prime Minister Winston Churchill, the whole of Great Britain might have unraveled long before the United States joined the war.

As important as these elements were to the people, there was George VI. England had a real king, not a Hollywood monarch. King George VI was not raised to the throne, but ascended to it in December of 1936 upon the abdication by his older brother, Edward, who relinquished the crown to marry divorcee Wallis Simpson, the woman he loved. George wore his crown reluctantly, overcoming a severe stammer to rally his people with heartfelt speeches. And when he was not speaking, his royal consort, Elizabeth, the Queen mother, did. When urged to allow her children to be taken from London to the safety of the provinces, she memorably proclaimed, "The children will not leave unless I do, I shall not leave unless their father does, and the King will not leave the country in any circumstances whatever."

And I should point out that this was years before MGM made "Mrs. Miniver."

We languished for many wet and noisy English months waiting for missions. *Combat America* was filmed but held up in post-production for reasons not explained to us at the time. Officers school and flight school were our official duties. Publicity was the unofficial duty. I can't lay claim to being worthy of either officer school or flight school; they were part of the deal cooked up by Metro to keep Gable out of danger. Getting a deal at all was an achievement. As much as President Roosevelt had insisted to Mr. Mayer that there was nothing he could do to keep Gable out of the service as long as he had enlisted, the President made a personal entreaty to the King to change his mind and keep making movies for the good of the war effort. Gable respectfully refused. There is no record of FDR's response.

In April of 1943, Clark and I were sent to Peterborough Army Base in England, a 400-acre expanse run by the RAF. We drove up to the gate and presented our orders to the guard who told us to report immediately to Colonel William Hatcher. "Just follow the signs," he said. "You'll see what I mean."

The first sign read "Welcome! Heavy Bombardment Group, First Air Division, Eighth Air Force." But the one that drew our attention was a smaller, hand-painted sign that had been nailed onto the post beneath the bigger one. It was a bird smoking a cigar, carrying a bomb, and dragging a banner reading "Home of Hatcher's Chickens."

"I hope it means hatching, like in eggs, and not chicken, like in coward," I said. "Or maybe it means we're all running around with our heads cut off. Or maybe even hatch like in booby hatch —"

Gable shut me down. "Shut up and keep your eyes on the road."

Here we go again, I thought. "I'm not the enemy, Clark, remember?"

"You'll do till Hitler shows up."

"Don't you think you're over-reacting a little?"

We rounded a corner and found Hatcher's office with ease; it was the one surrounded by photographers. Beside me, Clark gritted his teeth and said flatly but firmly, "Okay, Junior, go and do what you do best," and pushed me into the fray. Then he pasted a smile on his face, stepped out of the car, and acted like he wanted to see everyone, running headlong into the middle of the crowd.

Having heard about Fleet Street's penchant for aggressiveness, I pushed through the crowd speaking polite phrases like "'Scuse me," "Pardon me," "Sorry, chaps" and "Beg pardon" while using my elbows to pry the men apart and my arms to push them away. I had learned flanking techniques from Mannix's studio security force but this wasn't a premiere, it was a presentation of orders. I managed to clear a path for Clark to make it to the door of the building that held Hatcher's office. I thought I saw him look impressed with my skill, but it only lasted a blink as a blustery British woman in a severe suit strutted from the building and shoved me aside to face the equally surprised gaggle herself.

"All right, chaps, gangway," she said crisply, "it's only another soldier. The Colonel will be right out."

I pushed my way in front of her with a perfunctory "excuse me, Miss," and said, "I'm Alan Greenberg. I represent Metro-Goldwyn-Mayer and I'm in charge of Captain Gable."

She replied with equal assurance, "Mavis Roberts, Colonel Hatcher's civilian adjutant," and presented her hand to shake, "and I represent the British-American liaison. They told me you were being seconded to us."

"That's not the way I heard it."

She talked right through my protests. "Your client will stay standing here getting his picture taken until we bring him inside. Or would you rather find more ways to break protocol?"

I was about to say, "protocol isn't the only thing that's going to get broken around here" when Gable stepped between us and asked, "Do I shake hands or courtesy?"

"Neither," she said humorlessly, "you salute—the Colonel."

Which is exactly who appeared as if on cue. Hatcher stepped

from the doorway and strutted over to meet Gable with a firm salute and a handshake in his best Chamber of Commerce style. I saluted, too, and Hatcher ignored me.

"Captain Gable?" he said, "Bill Hatcher. Hatcher's Chickens. Heh heh. Welcome to the Chicken Coop."

"My compliments, sir," the King said. "General Arnold sends his as well."

"Aw, no need to bring ol' Hap into this, Clark," Hatcher said, presuming first-name with Gable and edging both of them around to give the photographers a better angle for their grip-and-grin photos. "This is our show now."

"Do you have a statement for the press?" one of the reporters asked.

"Yes I do," Hatcher said, "and it's also for the fine men serving here." He half-turned to the press and spoke, not to Clark, but past him, yet standing close by so any photo would have to include both of them. "Men, the enemy has asked for it. Give it to him. Seek no quarter beyond reason, Be firm, be just, and Godspeed to all of you." Then he said to Gable, not for public consumption, "Heh heh heh. You need anything, Mavis can find it." He leaned even closer to Gable and leered. "And I mean *anything*." Then he saw me. "Oh, but I forgot, you have an orderly."

Hatcher and Mavis stared at me as though I was something that just stuck to their shoes. It was going to be a long war

Chapter 11

April 3, 1943
First Air Div., England
Via V-mail
Howard Strickling, MGM Culver City

Dear Howard,

I'm finally able to write you a real letter instead of relying on the transatlantic cable, although these handwritten pages will be converted to V-mail Photostats to save weight and space. I'm going to be frank and pass the buck to you to decide how much, if anything, to release to Sime, Hedda, Louella, Jimmie, or any of our other friends in the press.

We have dug into our quarters in England. The men have already christened it "Uncle Bill and Tom's Contaminated Sack House." Clark is keeping mostly to himself as, every time he ventures anywhere, either in uniform or civvies, he is immediately recognized. It helps that he is a Captain so the enlisted men and lower-ranking officers and women don't bother him without cause. At present we are both waiting for an assignment. Clark has shot a picture called "Combat America" but for some reason its release has been delayed. Nothing to do with him, according to the scuttlebutt, but apparently it was caught in a pissing contest between two Army bureaucracies. Nothing like that could ever happen between producers at Metro, could it? The Army would love Clark to be in every frame, and if they order him to do so he will have to obey, but they are not stupid. They watch his reaction during planning meetings because they know that his enthusiasm is as important as his presence, and they don't want to squander one and lose the other. I asked him how he's holding up under all of this and he said, quote, "If I can survive Joan Crawford, Norma Shearer and George Cukor, the Army will be a piece of cake."

Our operation is called Hatcher's Chickens (not our choice) after the Colonel who runs the outfit, William Hatcher. He'd make a great character in a movie. He's flown just about everything with wings, treats everyone like a friend, and somehow manages to use Army inefficiency in his favor. For example, when he couldn't requisition a camera for some pick-up shots because they were all being held for an indefinite visit from a dignitary, he had me fill out separate requisitions for a lens, matte box, film magazine, viewfinder, pan head, and tripod — in short, everything for a camera except the camera itself — and when the Captain who'd made the bogus reservation discovered that all the parts had gone to Hatcher, he gave in and let Hatcher have the camera, too.

We are a section within a section. Somebody hung up a sign saying "The Little Hollywood Group." We not only get the mickey taken out of us because we're Yanks but also because we're Hollywood Yanks. The chief mickey-taker-outer is a veddy British lass named Mavis Roberts. Mrs. Miniver she's not. She goes out of her way not to go out of her way for us. She seems to be working for Hatcher in the same way I am working for you, which is to say, she won't say.

Gable looks fitter than ever. He's lost ten pounds, tightened up his already-taut body, and, because he's an officer, he is allowed to grow back his world-famous moustache. Because wartime security is being enforced on the base, he isn't bothered by members of the general public (not that the wonderfully reserved Brits would dare intrude on his privacy anyway), but he still draws stares from the servicemen and women because, let's face it, he is Clark Gable. He signs autographs if it doesn't disturb the goings-on but generally seeks a low profile. So far, he seeks it safely on the ground.

In addition to the King, our "little Hollywood group" includes the four guys we survived basic training with: Ronny Lewko, Victor Molina, Mike Battista, and Pete Jeffers. Apparently they all wanted to be airmen, but somehow they were sent to motion picture school and have stayed with us. Funny how the Army works just like a movie studio. Anyway, it was a gala reunion.

More later, Alan

BULLSHIT. IT WAS DAMN near a blanket party. The men thought Clark was responsible for killing their dreams of flying; Clark thought I was behind them wanting to stay with him; and I suspected Mavis was the mastermind until she proudly disclosed that it was part of General Arnold's plan to welcome Clark into the Hatcher's Chickens family. Personally, I thought it smacked of a bad casting decision but, whoever was behind it, it made for some interesting dynamics. The Yanks continued to give Clark the collective cold shoulder (Jeffers seemed to want to thaw but yielded to peer pressure). Mavis appointed herself the liaison between the King and the Colonel. Clark ignored it with practiced indifference, leaving me alone to pry everyone's knives out of my back. You were right; when in doubt, blame the publicist.

The most annoying part of all this is Mavis's idea that I am working for her and that if, perchance, she fails to get Clark to do something for her, he will do it for me, and orders me to persuade him. I tell her that it would be easier to get Leo the Lion to jump from Metro to Fox than to get Gable to follow my orders, but she is as persistent as Joan Crawford going after a role. This happened the other day.

"There's a radio broadcast tonight," she informed me at the last minute. "Toward the end of the hour they've cleared one minute for a public service announcement. Do you think you could get Captain Gable to make an appearance?"

"For what?" I asked.

"To remember to use the fat from chip fryers as long as you can, and then turn it over to the fat committee for the war."

"There's a fat committee?"

"Can you do it or not?"

"Try not to be so gracious," I said. "Let me check his schedule."

"Oh, he's free tonight after oh-sixteen hundred," Mavis knew.

"Since you've already cleared him, why not ask him yourself?"

"Because, strictly speaking, this isn't a military appearance. But it is for charity."

Something bugged me. "You've already asked him and he said no, didn't he?"

I knew that Mavis's silence meant Yes.

"You want me to get him to change his mind?" I chided.

"He never actually said no."

"Then what did he say? What *exactly?*"

"Um, he said I should ask you."

This was my opportunity. I could either chastise Mavis for pretending she was in charge or rib her for trying to save her ass by being coy. But what I truly felt was overriding pride that Clark would defer to me, even though he still didn't accept why I was there.

"All I can do is ask," I said. "I'll do what I can."

"Thank you, Alan," she said. I could have sworn that she dropped her guard for a split-second and actually looked approachable.

"Sure I'll do it, Junior," Clark said without hesitation when I asked him. "I woulda done it for Mavis, but I believe in going through channels."

The BBC had set up a field studio at the base and we did the cut-in without incident. That night I gained respect for radio technicians when I learned that that what sounds easy at home is terribly complicated in the doing. Cut-ins demand synchronized watches. There was no two-way communication between our field microphone and the BBC in London, so everyone hit "start" at the same time at the beginning of the show and, when it came your moment to speak, they flipped on the mike and you started talking, hoping that the folks on the other end had finished in time. It must have worked as planned because, the next day, both Clark and the Colonel got thank-you notes from the show's producer. Neither Mavis nor I got so much as a mention even though we set it up. If it had gone awry, of course, we would have been blamed. That's the joy of doing publicity.

Our "Little Hollywood Group" was becoming acclimated. One hazy morning, Clark was ensconced behind an anti-aircraft gun scanning the horizon for kraut bombers. The wind blew his hair in that rakish way Victor Fleming made it do in *Red Dust*. From Clark's expression, you'd think he was ready to take on the Luftwaffe single-handed. Then Mavis called for "one more please" and the Signal Corps photographer snapped another photo for the newspapers. Not only did the four guys from basic, who were standing around, shake their heads and chuckle, but two new members of our crew, Andriotti and Murtaugh, both of whom are actual combat veterans, actually had to stifle laughter. Mavis shot them a "you're not getting any tonight" look (which, from the way she acts toward all of us, was already obvious).

P.S. to Howard Strickling: The Army Air Corps is cutting Clark a lot of slack in what they ask him to do. They clearly want to make as much use of him as possible for recruiting purposes, but they are also sensitive to his whole reason for enlisting. I hear rumblings about sending him on "training" missions — that is, eyewash, in that would be set up to give him the experience of flying over enemy territory when, in fact, he would be going over areas that were pre-determined to be devoid of hostiles. Hitler's unstopped march through Europe and Scandinavia make this difficult to plan, but Hatcher is doing everything he can to mollify the King.

Gable continues to be a pro and a credit to Metro. If he feels bothered by the attention, he hides it, and I wouldn't blame him if he exploded one day. But so far he hasn't. Thank God Wally Beery didn't enlist.

Alan

Chapter 12

WHAT I DIDN'T DARE write Strickling about was the ongoing problem with Gable's fame. He might think that I couldn't deal with it. As it always is with people in our industry, the problem is seldom with the famous person, it's with other people's perception of it. Yet I don't hear about fans or photographers swarming around Jimmy Stewart, Robert Taylor, Henry Fonda, or other stars who serve in uniform.

I thought the barber's saving of Clark's hair trimmings was going to be the last of it, but there are scroungers in this man's Army that would make a Culver City dumpster diver feel naive. I happened to be standing in line behind Clark the other day when he handed his bed linens over at the to the Quartermaster to be laundered. "Just a minute," the intake man said, and started to unfold the sheets. It had pieces cut out of the middle of it.

"Moths?" he asked, suspiciously.

"No, Private," Clark told him. "Fans." It seems that civilian women had sneaked into his quarters and snipped souvenirs. "You can't always lock doors around here. Loose lips can sink ships, but loose locks turn Army issue bed sheets into cheesecloth."

"This is the third time this month," the laundry man said. "What are we gonna do?"

"Is there any way you can wash mine alone and give the same ones back to me?" Clark asked. To which I said, "What if word gets out that the King has his own fancy laundry service?"

"If we don't do something," Clark said, "before long I'll be sleeping on sheets the size of a handkerchief. You should have been in Atlanta for the world premiere of *Gone with the Wind*. The hotel chambermaids cut my sheets into one-inch squares and sold them for ten dollars each. They got fired, but they got rich."

"How many one-inch pieces can you get out of a bed sheet?" the laundry man asked.

"Who knows?" Clark said. "They probably even cut up six sheets that weren't mine before they were caught. They treated it like it was a piece of the true cross."

I had to marvel at the cleverness of it. As my mind careened through ways I could make a few extra bucks on it myself, Clark said, "Come on, Junior, let the poor guy do his job."

We were on the way to the production office when a group of girls rounded a corner and started giggling, a sure sign they recognized Gable.

"Keep walking," he said. "Don't make eye contact."

As we neared them, they grew silent. "Here it comes," Clark said. In an instant, we were surrounded. I was shoved aside, Clark twisted away to keep from being kissed by one of them, and another one, from out of nowhere, grabbed his uniform cap and took off. Then they all ran away to celebrate their prize.

"Is it like this all the time back home?" I asked.

"Not always," Clark said, quickly recovering from the attack. "When Carole and I go out —" he checked himself "—used to go out, we usually drove where we were going, say to a restaurant, and once we were inside it was normal. Oh, sure, we had fans waiting for us on the street — somehow they always know where you are — but they were always respectful. I gotta say that about the fans. The ones who just like you and your work are terrific. It's the shitheels who want something for themselves. The ones who shove pieces of paper in front of you and want your autograph. In a crowd, you never know what you're signing.

"People tended to leave Ma and me alone. They knew we were in love. That says something. I thought it would be different over here — British reserve and all that. And pretty much it has been when I go out, But when people get on the base, I guess they feel they're entitled. It's just the opposite at Metro. Inside the studio, you let people do their jobs."

By this time we had arrived at the office, which was next to Hatcher's in the temporary building. He opened a file drawer and inside there must have been five Keystone style uniform caps.

"Spares?" I asked.

"Spares," he said, putting a fresh one on. Then he winked at me. "Some time I'll show you where I keep my extra moustaches."

Clark may have warehoused hats, but I discovered that he seldom had to spend his own money when off the base. Although we had a fully stocked PX on the base, I was surprised when Clark would venture into the nearby village to buy cigarettes, toiletries, and the occasional tin of whatever food wasn't being rationed that week. I questioned why he would want to squander money at local shops when things cost so much less on base, and, moreover, weren't subjected to such strict rationing. "Why should I pay anything when I can get things for free?" he said. "I'll show you."

The next day he brought me along with him on a shopping trip.

Our first stop was a tobacconist where a lady clerk welcomed him with a cheerful familiarity. "What will it be today, Mr. Gable?" she asked.

"The usual," he said. "A pack of Lucky Strike Greens." The woman fetched a pack from the cabinet behind her and said, "that will be eighteen and a half p, Got a shilling, love?"

"Sorry, no," said Clark, smiling. "But I do have a cheque. Would you accept a personal cheque?"

"I always have before," she smiled back. It seemed like a ritual. He wrote his cheque for eighteen and a half pence, dated and signed it, blew the fountain pen ink dry, and handed it to her. "Cheerio," he added, putting the cigarettes in his pocket. I followed him out.

"I don't get it," I said. At the PX those would have cost you a nickel. You spent four times that."

"It's time you learned a few things that come along with fame, Junior," he said, spiriting me down an alley so he could light up. "You think it's all about getting good seats in restaurants. It is, but there's no free lunch once you get inside." He lit his cigarette. "Oh, sorry, you want one?" he offered. I waved it away and tried to stay upwind. "I learned this on my first publicity tour away from Los Angeles. Imagine you're a clerk in a drug store in Podunk. Clark Gable comes in for a pack of Luckys. He pays by check. A signed check that has his autograph on it. Are you ever going to cash that check?"

My face was answer enough.

"You can't do it for big items. If you want a new washer or a car, you have your agent contact the manufacturer and you pose for a newspaper ad. I never have, but a lot of them do. I just do it for pissy items like cigarettes and shaving cream. Maybe fish and chips. Never for personal services like shoe shines or tips, 'cause those guys need the cash, but merchandise, hell yes. In Hollywood everybody's too jaded to give any of us a freebie, but everywhere else? It's the one perk I don't mind taking advantage of. It makes up for a lot of torn clothes, shredded sheets, and stolen hats."

As we returned to the base, I felt ashamed of all the 8x10 photos I'd stolen from the studio files and forged people's name on to sell for a dollar. If I got back alive, I vowed to charge at least five dollars.

Chapter 13

ONE FRIDAY NIGHT I decided to try my hand at creating team spirit. I was fed up with the way Clark — and, let's face it, I, too — were being shut out of the ever-tightening circle of Lewko, Molina, Jeffers, Battista, and, more recently, Andriotti and Murtaugh. They weren't doing anything grandiose like pushing us in front of on-coming traffic. It was subtle things like finding six seats together at the mess hall instead of eight (Clark refused to dine in the officers' mess) or saying they were going to the movie show and then leaving together after the newsreel to head somewhere else. For all the effort they went through to shun us, wouldn't it have been easier to get along? But I guess it made them feel more, I dunno, special.

I decided to ignore that and find a way for all of us to show our solidarity before heading into our first battle. I figured that would be better than having to bond in a hurry during aerial shelling. It shouldn't have been my call -— after all, it was Hatcher who had the bright idea to put all his chickens in one coop -— but, as I have often found with producers, the idea itself is more important to them than the details of how to pull it off.

I was in the production office writing a progress report to send to Metro. Gable sat across the room at his desk. I had to look busy.

He didn't. All he had to do was be Clark Gable. What he would rather have been doing was flying over occupied Europe dropping bombs on Nazis, but you can't have everything.

My reports to Metro, as shown before, weren't exactly lying, but they weren't exactly telling the truth, either. Candor is fine in the abstract but is seldom appreciated in the particular, especially in Hollywood. For example, when we screen a new film and it's a turkey, we can't call it what it is: a dud, a stiff, a loser, etc. Everybody in the screening room knows damn well that it has feathers and gobbles, but we all have to play the game. That's when the euphemisms start. "It's a special picture," someone will say. "It will need careful handling," says someone else. A third offers, "We'll have to reach out to the audience that can appreciate it." But all the soft soap adds up to the same thing: we're going to waste a month and spend a lot of favors pushing a piece of shit on an unsuspecting public.

Fortunately, we can still make money off bad pictures. This is because Loew's, Incorporated, Metro's parent company, owns the major theatre circuit in America. We play our movies in our theatres. In cities where we don't have screens, we have deals with the other exhibition chains where they have to take all our pictures, including the duds, if they want to get the good ones. The slang for this is "block booking," but our sales department prefers the term "playing a season." It simplifies the scheduling of an entire year's releases even before they're made. Independent theatre owners are always complaining that they're at a disadvantage. They ask why they can't just book the good pictures. How would that leave us when we have a whole slate to sell? I suppose they'll take us to court some day over it, but right now it pays the rent and keeps a few thousand people employed fifty-two weeks a year.

My train of thought was derailed by a crumpled wad of paper hitting me in the nose.

"Who are you always writing to, Junior?" Gable's voice asked from across the room. "Some girl back home?"

"Yeah, that's it," I lied, and quickly took my Metro report out of the typewriter to mail later.

"How'd you meet a dame?"

"The usual way," I said.

"Did you meet her on the lot? Is she some young starlet?"

"I have a life outside of the studio, you know," I acted offended.

"Tell me about her." The King was pushing.

"I believe it's vulgar for two guys to sit around discussing women," I risked.

"And I do believe you're ducking the question. All right, Junior, I'll play it your way. Is there one girl or do you play the field?"

"Hey," I said, acting sassy, "I may not be Clark Gable, but I get around."

"Sure," he said. "But what about around here? I never see you go out on leave. A big night for you is staying on the base and watching a Betty Grable movie."

"Have you ever met Betty Grable?" I asked.

"Don't change the subject," Clark said. Then he looked playful. "I'll bet you're stuck on that Mavis Roberts gal."

"I'd rather go down on Marie Dressler," I said.

"She's dead," he said.

"I'd *still* rather go down on her."

"Mavis is your type, Junior." He wouldn't let up.

"I don't exactly see you going out with anyone," I said. The moment the words came out, I wish they hadn't.

He spoke softly. "I don't think I'm ready for that yet."

This was my chance. "Maybe there's something you *are* ready for," I said, not pausing. "Seven-thirty at The Red Lion Pub. If we don't date, we can at least drink. Or, as they say here, half-seven at the local."

"What's there?" he asked.

"Beer, smoke, and noise," I said. "I'll even get Metro to pick up the tab. We can celebrate."

"Celebrate what?"

"I'm sure we'll find something after our fifth or sixth pint."

"Who's this 'we' you keep talking about."

"You still don't trust me?"

Silence.

"Seven-thirty at The Red Lion. I've told the guys. Don't make me look like the liar you think I am."

To make the point, I picked up the wad of paper and threw it back at him. Effortlessly, he backhanded it across the room.

The Red Lion was the perfect local. Situated within staggering-home distance of Peterborough, it had somehow arranged dispensation from the Licensing Board to expand its hours. There must have been some kind of outside deal, too, because there was an MP station practically next door to The Red Lion, just in case. On the wall were signs in American English ranging from "watch your wallets" to "that lass may be an Axis spy" and every warning or health prohibition in between. Unlike bars in the States, there was no live music, just drinks, and not normal drinks, but carefully controlled portions served by the barman or barmaid from a device called an optic. It was an upside-down bottle nestled in a dispenser with a spring-loaded valve. You pushed the glass up against it and it let out a one-ounce portion. Hard liquor was drunk at room temperature. No ice. Beer — called bitters — was also drunk at room temperature. The difference, which I noticed immediately, was that English beer tasted like you always imagined beer was supposed to taste, and therefore could be enjoyed practically warm, whereas you began to understand why American beers needed to be chilled for consumption. As the joke went, an American brewery needed to get government certification before selling its product, so they sent a sample of their beer to Washington to be tested. Two weeks later they received a letter saying, "We regret to inform you that your horse has diabetes."

Ronny Lewko, Victor Molina, Mike Battista, and Pete Jeffers were holding a table when I got there early enough to try to hold a table first. I had no illusions about the group of us becoming close friends, but I knew that, if any of them made it back to the states, the press would milk them for every dram of gossip about Clark, and I wanted them to feel invested in his image. I didn't care if they thought I was an asshole. The King came first.

Lewko was the ringleader. He looked like he fell off a Wheaties box. He reminded me of the quarterback on the high school football team, the one who got all the girls, all the applause, all the privileges, and then wound up working in a filling station after graduation. From his name, I figured him for Polish, and when he was around I never felt so Jewish in my life. He kept distant, probably because he had some kind of chip on his shoulder I couldn't figure.

I don't know where in Italy Victor Molina's people came from. I just wondered how they managed not to wind up in Brooklyn. Instead, when they got off the boat a generation ago, they went straight to Little Italy in lower Manhattan. Jews and Italians have everything in common except religion. We share guilt, family unity, and an insistence that only our mothers know how to cook food right. All Molina ever talked about was all the girls he had enjoyed back home. Every time he recounted a conquest, I got the odd feeling that I had seen the same thing in a movie. Finally I realized that, instead of being discreet when he said, "and you can imagine what happened next," he was actually describing how the scene in the movie faded out, and he really didn't have a clue about what happened next. I let him have his fantasy by not telling him I'd seen the same movie before it was censored by the Breen Office.

Miguel Battista was an enigma. He insisted we call him "Mike," probably in an attempt to sound more American, but this was useless because his face was a map of Havana. He didn't get along too well with Molina; something to do with a blood feud that started centuries ago in the Mediterranean that nobody remembered except that it was crucial to keep it alive. Battista was always asking me about various states. For some reason he assumed that, because I moved from New York to California, I had stopped in all forty-eight of them along the way. He'd never left New York, but he wanted to know about Kansas, Kentucky, Mississippi, and any place else that anyone might hail from. At the same time, he already seemed to know a great deal about them. Turns out he used to read the WPA guides to the states. His curiosity and thirst for knowledge was remarkable, especially given the yahoos he hung around with. I made a mental note to stay in touch with him if we made it through the war.

The one I had the most hope for bringing over to my side was Pete Jeffers. He'd already dropped his guard by recognizing Gable and asking me a few fan questions. He was the emblem of Clark's fan base: the kind of guy who'd love to join Gable on hunting trips or for a beer and wouldn't feel ditched when women came up and wanted the King's attention. Jeffers could be my wedge into Lewko, Molina, and Battista. He could tell them that Gable was an okay fellow and to stop giving him grief for being famous. I never knew what town in Michigan Jeffers was from — it clearly wasn't Detroit — but it had to have had a romanticized world view. In other words, he was the typical ticket-buying public, God bless 'em.

There was a sixth finger I'd added to tonight's revelry. I recruited him from another unit. Paul Harding was a baby-faced bruiser who could have figured in an MGM cartoon as the big galoot of a bulldog who gives Tom the Cat a hard time. I felt for him. In grade school he was probably the kid who everybody thought was a bully, even though he wasn't. Little kids probably picked on him because they knew he wouldn't dare hit them back. He was tall, fleshy (even after fourteen weeks of basic), and had a sweet face. Naturally, I hired him to start a fight. That was my plan. He'd lean on Clark, I'd try to make him stop, and the other guys would form bonds coming to the rescue. I was sure it would work, just like it did in every movie ever made.

I gave the barmaid an order for another round of drinks and carried them to the table to set them up. As I handed them around, Jeffers was finishing a story. "I heard when he took off his shirt in *It Happened One Night* and was bare-chested, undershirt sales dropped fifty percent." He looked at me to confirm it. I let it hang in the air.

"I still wear one," Battista boasted.

"Who cares?" Lewko said. "They make us all wear them."

Jeffers was still impressed with his own story. "Fifty percent!"

This time I bit. "That's what they say, gentlemen, only I never believe the publicity. Thank you for coming."

"What for?" Molina said, already slurring his words. "You buyin'?"

"No, *you're* buying," I said. "Not the beer, the publicity. The undershirt thing, that's a fake statistic."

"It is?" said Jeffers. He seemed hurt. "I read it in the paper. If it's in the paper, it has to be true."

I was feeling my oats. "Who do you think put it there?"

Lewko had to score one against Jeffers. "See?" Then, to me, "Who? You?"

"No," I said, raising my glass, "but here's to the movies. Make you laugh, make you cry, kiss your two bits goodbye."

Lewko downed his pint in five seconds. We all marveled. "Okay," he said, and belched. "That's the stuff that guys like you put in the paper. Tell us about the stuff that you keep out of the papers."

I played dumb. "What stuff?"

"Tell us all about Jean Harlow and Joan Crawford and all the women who come out to Hollywood to be stars and — "

I broke in. "Pete, Pete, back off. The last thing Gable wants to talk about is movies. He's given enough interviews to last a lifetime. So unless he brings it up himself, no dropping hints, just try to remember what I —"

They all stopped listening and turned toward the door. I was expecting Clark. Instead, it was Mavis.

"Shit," I said. "The redcoats are coming."

Chapter 14

I GOT UP SO fast I knocked my chair over. That, of course, drew Mavis's attention straight to me. I met her midway. "What are you doing here?"

"In case you forgot, you signed out to this address," she said haughtily.

"You're not invited. This is guys' night at the local."

"And I thought I'd join you. As see from the sign, ladies are invited"

"It wasn't an invitation and this isn't publicity."

"If you make headlines, it will be."

"We don't intend to make anything, Miss Roberts," I said. "This is called R&R — rest and relaxation. I assume you've heard of the concept even if you don't practice it."

"Not until the war is over, Mr. Greenbaum."

"Greenberg, and listen up, Miss Tightarse. It's because of your little announcement not to treat Captain Gable any differently that he's become a piece of meat on display ever since we got here. I had hoped that your country's famous sense of propriety would leave him alone, but no. Well, tonight I've got these guys primed to forget he's famous and we don't need you."

"Are you trying to hurt my feelings?"

"If you have any. How am I doing?" I couldn't believe I was saying this to a woman, but she wasn't a woman, she was a fellow publicist encroaching on my territory.

"Primed?" she challenged, "or paid? Are you paying these young men to make nice?"

"As long as it's not the Chancellor of the Exchequer picking up the tab, what do you care?"

"Very good," she cooed. "At least your making an effort to understand our country. Now, quick, who's the Archbishop of Canterbury?"

"Thomas Becket. Don't tell the king."

Before she could dredge up a witty anti-yank answer, Harding sidled up like a sheepdog trying to get my attention. "Excuse me, sir, but when do I bust in?"

Mavis didn't know what to make of this, but I could see the tumblers turning. "This is getting interesting," she said. "Mind if I watch?"

"A couple of minutes after he gets here," I told Harding, ignoring Mavis. "And for God's sake don't get a real buzz on. He's in better shape than you are."

"Better shape than me?" the gentle giant said. "You think so? Here, feel that." He flexed his biceps at Mavis. "Go ahead and squeeze 'em, lady."

She had no hesitation wrapping both hands around his arm. They didn't reach. "Lovely," she said to him while looking at me. "I bet all the girls love you."

"I wouldn't know, ma'am," he said shyly. "But I'd shore like to find out." By now Mavis could see the writing and backed off wordlessly.

"What did I say?" Harding asked, looking hurt.

"Nothing Paul, it wasn't your fault. Miss Roberts was leaving anyway. You wait at the bar and keep drinking those Cokes." I nudged him away and turned to the others, who were enjoying the show.

"Here's the plan," I began. Mavis watched. "I've asked Clark to join us." There was general grumbling. "I know, I know," I continued, "but cut him some slack, wouldja? Ever since boot camp he's tried time and again to be normal. He's not the one making a thing out of this, you are. I'll pay you each a fiver. That's five pounds apiece, that' almost fifteen dollars in American. Just be nice to him tonight. You don't have to blow smoke up his ass, but he's a really good guy if you give him half a chance." I took out six crisp five pound notes and handed them around. The men pocketed them.

"Did he ask you to do this?" Lewko asked.

"No!" I answered quickly. "He doesn't know anything about it. Now c'mon. The drinks are free; you can at least play along. For one night, one night, that's all I'm asking. You might even have a good time if you'd take your thumbs out of your asses long enough —." Immediately I could see that they were no longer looking at me. They were staring past me toward the entrance.

Gable had arrived. He was immaculately dressed in civvies, polished shoes, trousers crisply pressed. And this is important: he shifted his weight, didn't make eye contact with anyone, slouched slightly, and, as we watched, the biggest movie star in the world become completely anonymous. No one in The Red Lion but us looked at him. Stars can do that.

He came directly to the table and shook hands all around as if he was meeting them for the first time. "Hi," he said, "Clark

Gable." He called each of them by name and effortlessly de-fused any negative reaction. Stars can do that, too. "Jeez, Alan, why didn't you say it was a Board meeting of the Little Hollywood group. Hiya, Ronny. Hey, Victor. Hi, Mike. Hiya, Pete. For a while I was worried this was gonna be some kind of surprise party."

"Hi, Captain Gable," Molina managed.

"Off duty it's Clark, Victor. Or is it Vic?"

"Whatever's good for you."

It went like that. "See, that wasn't so hard. The way you guys avoided me, you'd think I had cooties."

Rather than wait for an awkward pause, I stepped right in. "I figured if we're all gonna fly together we ought to get acquainted somewhere other than the barracks or the mess hall."

"Tell that to the Army," Molina groused. "Sure we're supposed to fly together, but they won't say when. We're supposed to do something but they won't say what. We've been shooting film of maneuvers for the last, what, eight or nine months, and we're still waiting to be put on one of our own. You think it's because they don't want anything to happen to you, Captain — I mean Clark?"

"Sure feels like it to me," Clark groused back. "The Colonel said as much."

"The Army sure does things bass-ackwards," Lewko said.

Jeffers looked around. "Careful. Loose lips sink ships."

"Why?" Lewko said. "Torpedoes don't have lips. Do they?"

Gable laughed.

Lewko laughed too. "I made a joke?"

"Naw, I just got it," Gable said. "Hatcher's Chickens. I'll tell you what kind of hatch it is. It's a booby hatch!"

Everyone laughed. Five seconds too long. Forced. Gable sensed it and let the table calm down naturally before he started a story.

"You know I like to hunt. A lot of us do, but we only get to go out between pictures, and a lot of us are kept busy. I'm going out duck hunting with Howard Hawks and he calls and asks if it's okay if William Faulkner tags along. Howard and Bill are writing a picture for Bogart and Bacall, see. We're waiting there in the duck blind and after a while the conversation turns to books. Faulkner says, 'There's only five good writers working now: Willa Cather, Ernest Hemingway, John dos Passos, Thomas Mann, and me.' And I say, 'Oh, do you write, Mr. Faulkner?' and he says, 'Yes. And what do you do, Mr. Gable?'"

Everyone laughed but Lewko, who gave it a try, but got lost. "Who's William Faulkner?"

Jeffers knew. "You maroon, he's a writer."

"Like what?" Lewko pressed. Suddenly I couldn't think of a single title.

"*Sanctuary, Absalom-Absalom, As I lay Dying,*" Battista listed. When he felt the others' stares burning into him, he stopped. "Um, I like to read a lot," he said to the floor.

"I hunt possum," Lewko said. "Back home, I mean. Whatta y'all shoot?"

"Griffin and Howe .30/06 mostly," Gable said. Lewko was impressed.

"First rifle my daddy got me was a .22."

"That's what I gave my wife," Clark said. "She hated it, wanted to try mine. So I let her. First time she fired my .30/06 it knocked her flat on her ass. After that, she—." He grew silent. The clouds were gathering again. This time Jeffers read the signals.

"Hey, I thought we came here to drink!" He shoved his untouched pint in front of Clark. Clark pushed it back.

"Thanks, but I think I'll pass."

And here is where Harding staggered up. I couldn't tell if he was really drunk or just pretending, but he had no idea how bad his timing was.

"Well if it ain't the big movie star!" he slurred. "Who do you think you are, Rhett Butler?"

I tried to signal him to pull it back but he was into full performance mode. Fortunately, Gable was used to things like this. "Aw, he's just havin' a good drunk."

Harding didn't get it and, instead, said, "'Smatter, too famous to look a member of the public in the eye?"

I smiled up at him. "I don't think we need you to do this any more."

"Shut up," he hissed and I smelled liquor on his breath. He was drunk. Probably had to knock back a few to get his nerve up, and then went over the edge. Instead of biting, Gable glanced casually up at him, not raising his voice, but looking at the poor kid straight-on. "Young man, I'd ask you to join us but this is a private gathering. I'd be happy to buy you a drink at the bar if you like."

Harding searched for an insult. "Oh yeah?" he said, "let's see the South rise again after *this*, mister movie star!"

Now I gave him a stage whisper, "All right, enough."

"He'll go away," Gable said, "just ignore him."

Wrong. "Oh yeah?" Harding shouted. "Ignore this!"

Harding put his hand on Gable's shoulder to spin him around, but Gable reached back and yanked Harding's legs out from under him, sending him backward to the floor.

All of The Red Lion now got quiet and looked. All they saw, however, was Clark Gable rising from his chair to magnanimously lift a passed-out G.I. to his feet and give him his chair. "Okay, son, you win. How about joining us for a pint? Say hi to the boys." He introduced all of us and then held out his hand to the stunned Harding. "And I'm Clark."

"And I'm Paul Harding," Harding said weakly.

"Save my place, Paul," Clark said, heading off to the loo. "I gotta piss."

Harding looked around at us, then off as Gable retreated. "Holy shit, do you know who that is?"

Gable stood at the urinal trough in the gents room doing his business when a sailor wobbled in and stood next to him, staring straight ahead. Then he started to list to the left and Gable grabbed his tunic with his free hand. Next, he listed to the right and Gable pushed him back. "Steady ahead, Admiral," Gable chided. The sailor turned to see who was talking. His eyes turned as big as portholes at the sight of the King.

"Holy shit," he said. "You're Clark Gable."

"Yes," Gable said, "And you're three sheets to the wind." With that, the kid turned his whole body in Gable's direction and saluted. At the same time, he peed all down the star's trouser leg.

"Hey," Clark said, "hard to port!" He twisted the kid back toward the trough and made for the wash basin, but it was too late. One pant leg and shoe had been doused.

Gable left the loo and made for the table in time to see all the guys returning the fivers I had paid them to be nice. Each of them made it a point to say it was a point of honor to give the money back and that Gable was a great guy and they couldn't accept money. But what Clark saw was me collecting money and thought that I was demanding payoffs to be in his company.

By the time he got to the table he was purple with rage. "What the hell is this, Greenberg? You selling tickets to me?"

"No, Clark. We're just splitting the tab."

"I don't believe you."

"It's true," Lewko attempted. "We're all kicking in for beers."

He turned to Harding, who was still seated and still baked. "How much did he pay you to try and pick a fight with me, Harding?"

"Nothing, sir." A pause. "Okay, five pounds, but I spent it or I'd give it back like the others." Another pause. "Wow, you remembered my name."

Gable didn't believe him. "I can make my own friends, see? Nobody has to buy 'em for me. Least of all some junior publicist."

"Wait, Clark," I protested. "You've got it all wrong."

"It's Captain Gable from now on, Greenberg."

Then there was a voice behind all of us. "Oh, it's Captain Gable now, is it? Or should that be Captain Lame-ass Movie Star?"

Clark turned. It was Daly, our drill sergeant from Florida. Somehow he had been assigned to England, and here he was, shitfaced.

"You shtill think you're special?" he challenged from his cups.

Gable jerked his thumb toward me while looking at Daly. "How much are you paying this asshole?"

I shook my head. "Nothing. Comes naturally to him."

The glow of opportunity lit up Clark's face. The two men seemed evenly matched, except one of them was an officer and the other was not. One of them was also famous and the other was drunk. But here they were out of uniform and off duty.

Whoever blinked first would lose.

Chapter 15

I HAD TO ADMIRE the drill sergeant. All along I'd thought he was just a dumb bully. Turns out he was a clever strategist. He correctly figured that if he could goad Clark into taking a pop at him, even if Clark decked him, Gable would lose in the press. And if he hit first he would get a wash because everyone knows that movie stars are violent, demanding egotists. That's why he stood three inches off Clark's nose and sprayed his 3.2 beer breath onto the King's trimmed moustache.

You have to drink a lot of 3.2 beer to get drunk, and Sergeant Daly did his duty. "Nobody paid me shit," he said, "and that's more'n your kisser's worth, dickhead. Nothing but shit."

Gable gave him the same insulting leer he gave Norma Shearer in *Idiot's Delight* but said, benignly, "You'll never get that one past the Hays Office.' Then he said to me — again without taking his eyes off the drunken Daly — "Why don't you go next door and get the MPs? I have a feeling our friend here is going to require their presence." I began to leave but the sergeant threw out his arm and blocked me.

"This little Yid stays where he is 'cause he's next."

Gable addressed the others. "This mug's had a hard-on for me ever since basic. I'm no stranger to guys who get a little taste of power and then use it to make other people miserable. Where I come from, they're called producers. The difference is, if I slug a producer, I get put on suspension but everybody I work with pats me on the back. But if I slug him, I look like the heavy. So let's put it to a vote. What do you say?"

The whole pub had ideas. "Slug him," was one. "Just leave him," ran second. I thought other fights were going to break out over it. It got so bad that Sergeant Daly didn't know whose orders to follow. Half the pub wanted to see Gable level him, the other half wanted to do it themselves. Finally Gable just shook his head in pity and started to leave peacefully. "If you were half the man you think you are, you woulda hauled off by now and —" He never finished the sentence. Daly roundhoused him with all his might, but only caught the back of Clark's head and he spun around and down to the floor. When Gable saw what happened, he reached down, picked up the drill sergeant with his left hand, stood him up so he balanced, and — I swear this is true — took one finger, placed it on his forehead, and pushed him ass-over-teakettle across the table. Daly crumpled like the sack of shit he was (do I sound biased?).

It was as though a director called "action." Everybody in The Red Lion had been watching Gable all along, and this was like a signal for the stuntmen to take the field. Only these weren't stuntmen, they were professionally trained, combat-ready men from all of the services, and if they couldn't take a swing at Hitler, by God, they were going to flatten each other.

Almost immediately, someone picked up a wooden stool and brought it across my back. The pain was blinding. "What the hell was that for?"

Gable called out to me, "The real ones don't break away, Junior," as he ducked a punch from the sailor who'd just pissed on his pants and was getting his second wind. The publican reached for the phone to call the

MPs, who were just next door, but had to let it go to dodge an incoming ash tray. "Hey, mate," he shouted, "that's the twenty-year-old Scotch!"

Drunks get inventive. One dogface stood and shouted, "Ten Hut!" as though an officer had just entered. Anybody who fell for it got slugged by the G.I. nearest to him.

Of our Little Hollywood Group, Gable was doing his best to push away anyone who wanted to have at him. Generally, he handed them off to Lewko who punched them with unerring precision; Molina ducked whenever he could; and Battista got in a few jabs. The one to watch was Harding who, it developed, could absorb any number of hits until his opponent tired, and then he brought his meaty fist down on the poor guy's head like a carnival hammer, knocking him cold.

I did what I could from under the nearest table. All of a sudden Gable leaned down, grabbed me by the collar, and asked, "How many friends did you hire? Come clean."

"None of them," I said. "I mean, I did at first, but when you went off to piss they all said what a great guy you are and made me take the money back. You saw half of it and thought they were bribing me."

The sound of police whistles filled the room and the fighting stopped. Four MPs entered, spaced themselves across the front, and secured the room.

"Ten SHUN!" the tallest one said. "Who started this?"

Gable stood up. "I did."

The MP walked to Gable. You could see him recognize Clark, then check out everybody else in the room, then back at Clark. "I guess you better come with me, sir," he said.

Then Lewko said, "He didn't start it, Officer. I did."

"No he didn't. I did," added Molina. Soon half the guys in the place confessed. It was like Spartacus, with liquor.

The MP sighed. "Is there anybody here who *didn't* start it?"

"Yeah," said the drill sergeant. He pulled himself to his feet, brushed himself off, glared at Gable, and said, "I got blindsided by Rhett Butler."

The MP pushed his Billie club into Daly's stomach. "And I got kissed by the Wizard of Oz. Come with us."

"I didn't do anything!"

"Did you wake up this morning?" the MP asked.

"Of course."

"That's enough for me." He put cuffs on him. "You were my drill sergeant in boot camp. I can't wait to get you in the brig."

While everybody watched the drill sergeant's chickens come home to roost, I pulled Gable aside. "This won't last." I led him toward the back door. On the way out, we passed a case of bottles. Gable grabbed one and followed me into the alley. As soon as we stepped off the curb, the sailor from the bathroom ran up to us as though something was wrong. You could see the fear in his eyes.

"What's wrong, son?" Gable said, grabbing the kid by the shoulders.

"I'm gonna be sick," he said, and barfed all over my shoes. As I stood in a pool of Navy puke, Gable uncorked the bottle he'd liberated and handed it to me. "Here's your chaser." I took two swigs.

"What is it?" I asked.

"What does the bottle say?"

"Mortlach single malt," I managed to read through the tears gathering in my eyes.

"Are you a Scotch whiskey man?" Gable asked, "because that's about the best you can get." He grabbed the bottle from me and sucked down a generous swig.

"It's wasted on me," I confessed. "I've never been a drinker and, if you don't believe me, I'll prove it to you."

"Well I am," Gable said, kissing the bottle and taking another drink. "I haven't done this since I enlisted and I think it's about time. You can drive."

"I don't have a car."

"Get a taxi."

"I smell like puke."

"I told you not to drink."

Three taxis later (we were kicked out of the first two; the third driver had a cold) we made it back to the Officers Quarters. By then Clark was feeling no pain and the bottle had given up its ghost. As I eased Clark into his cot, he said, "Where you from, sailor?"

"The U.S.S. Budweiser."

By now Gable had settled into a cozy drunk. His face was red but, for the first time I could remember, it was relaxed. If the Lord protects a drunk, He really goes out of His way to protect a drunk movie star. Lieutenants, however, aren't as charmed. I tiptoed to the head and wiped off my government-issued shoes. When I got back to check on Gable, he mumbled, "I hereby rescind my earlier order and authorize you to call me 'Clark' again."

"I disobeyed that order four drinks ago," I said. "By the way, we get up at six AM, which is three hours from now, and I will be very happy to see you standing in front of a camera and a machine gun, both of which will be as loaded as you are right now."

Clark started waving his arms like he was batting away flies.

"Cameras! Cameras! Why cameras?"

I'd had enough for the fifth time tonight. "Because you're a movie star, stupid."

"I deserve it," he said. "Do you believe a guy like me in movies? I'm just a lucky slob from Ohio who happened to be at the right place at the right time. I can't act worth a damn, can't do half the stuff they want, but somehow it works."

"Of course it works. You're the King."

He stopped fanning the air and covered his face. "What good's a King without his Queen?"

Gable reached into his open shirt and lifted his dog tags from around his neck. Fastened with them on the chain was a small gold box. I thought he was holding it up for me to look at, but he brushed my hand away. "When Ma's plane crashed into the mountain," he said thickly, "I tried to go up and find her. They wouldn't let me. Held me back. I said I knew it was bad. They said it was worse than I knew." His eyes grew moist. "I never should have let her go."

"It wasn't your fault, Clark. I keep telling you."

"Inside this box — Ma's earrings — first anniversary — she was wearing 'em when she — they found 'em. This is all I have left of Ma." He managed to focus on me. He dropped the amulet back on his chest and soft-punched me on my chin. "You're all right, Junior." Then he passed out.

"You know your problem, Clark?" I said as his snoring started. "Your problem is you don't have a problem. Everybody else does. And that's a problem."

I turned off the bed stand lamp, grabbed my shoes, and went outside in my socks. It was just past three A.M.

When I hit the steps, a fully uniformed and crisply presented Mavis was waiting for me. "All right, then," she said, "you want to talk? Let's talk."

Chapter 16

JUST AFTER I STARTED at Metro I got a call to bring some Myrna Loy head shots down to stage fourteen for her to sign. When I got there, they were setting up for the next shot and Miss Loy was relaxing in a secluded corner of the stage, not her regular bungalow across the lot. The first time you're in a Hollywood soundstage, what strikes you is its vastness, like an airplane hangar. You have to be careful not to touch anything, even what looks like it might be in the way, because it could be part of a "hot set," that is, something that is still being used and must remain in continuity.

The second time you walk into a Hollywood soundstage, you curse the vastness because it takes forever to get anywhere and you want to get back to what you were doing before they called and said to get right over. I had ten Mickey Rooneys waiting on my desk to get out to his fan club and a Spencer Tracy that needed a legitimate autograph.

I knocked on a wooden strut that was holding the curtain across Miss Loy's alcove and heard "come in" but, when I went in, the only person inside was her stand-in. "Here are the pictures for Miss Loy," I said, and the assistant took them. Not only that, she sat down at the vanity and started to sign them herself. (I watched over her shoulder; her forgery was better than mine.) Almost immediately, the assistant director stuck his head in and said, "We're ready for you, Miss Loy." To my astonishment, the stand-in answered, "Thank you, Russ," and got up, handing me the pictures. "Could you bring these to the stage? I'll finish signing them between takes."

I followed her to the set, which was ready to roll. She took her mark, the make-up woman did a few touch-ups, and the juicers turned the full lighting grid back on. Within seconds I saw the shadows falling the right way, the halo light hitting her from behind, and the key light bringing out the shape of her perfect pug nose. Faster than you can say "Hollywood magic," the woman I thought was the stand-in became Myrna Loy.

I'm not saying that Myrna Loy wasn't beautiful, charming, and poised. I'm saying that she was something beyond beautiful, charming, and poised. I'm saying it was that "something extra" that the camera truly does love, and it took Hollywood to bring it out.

I'm saying all of this because, when Mavis Roberts stepped into the moonlight, she wasn't Myrna Loy, but she wasn't Zasu Pitts, either. It was just after three A.M., and I was definitely sober. The dawn was many hours away, and the stairwell was dark. The foggy English climate gave her that perfect skin, and the moonlight made it glow. I thought I saw her resolute expression soften into something approaching, well, approachability. Or maybe I was still a little drunk.

"I've been waiting for you to return," she said, leading me out to the road. "I couldn't sleep. I had to clear something up."

"Do you always sleep in business clothes?" I asked.

"I didn't change for bed," she said, "I sat up."

"Well, here I am. What's on your mind?"

She cleared her throat, which signaled a rehearsed spiel. "As you know, Captain Gable is as important to the Army as he is to MGM. You happen to work for one, I happen to work for the other. "

I decided to derail her before she got started. "Why not just admit it: your job is to exploit Gable as much as you can. My job is to protect MGM's investment and look after a man who has become my friend. I have more at stake in this than you do."

She got flustered. "What's at stake, Leftennant (sic) Greenbaum is winning the war. May I finish?"

"Greenberg. Go ahead."

"The moment Captain Gable enlisted, he was assigned here. They may not have given you those orders, but they gave them to the Colonel and I. Rather, the colonel and me."

"Hey, why do you say 'leff-tenant' when it's spelled 'loo-tenant?'"

"Because I speak English."

"Then why don't you call it the leff instead of the loo?"

"For the same reason we call them 'chips' instead of 'French fries,' the 'boot' instead of the 'trunk,' and it's bloody well 'over here' instead of 'over there' where it should have stayed."

"Do you know that the moonlight makes you look different?"

"Moonlight does strange things, Lieutenant. It almost makes you look sober."

I locked my eyes onto hers and said nothing. It's an old trick I learned interviewing new contract players. If you don't say anything after they give you their prepared answer, they sometimes get nervous and start talking again, this time with the truth. Mavis must have known the same trick, because we stood there like two andirons. I thought I felt her sway a little toward me, so I swayed a little toward her. "Alan," she said seductively, and I stopped. She lowered her voice. This was it. And then she said, "You have a meeting with the Colonel at oh-six hundred hours. Do you want me to knock you up?"

I couldn't believe what I was hearing. "Do we have time? Do you have a place?"

She rolled her eyes. "Oh, God, you Americans. 'Knock you up' is British for 'wake-up call.'"

I couldn't help it: "Honey, you're the one who needs a wake-up call."

She smiled, but it wasn't an inviting smile, it was a "I won that point" smile. "Good morning, Loo-tenant Greenberg," she said, did a British about-turn (instead of an American about-face) and no doubt headed back to her native earth before the sun came up.

I knew she liked me. What was worse, I thought I liked her.

When I got to my quarters it wasn't even worth going to sleep, so I showered, shaved, and wrote another letter to Metro.

April 20, 1943
First Air Div., England
Via V-mail
Howard Strickling, MGM Culver City

Dear Howard,

We have our first mission briefing in a few hours. I can't say more about it for security reasons. This is where I will learn how serious Gable is about flying over enemy territory, how serious the Army Air Corps is about letting him, and how seriously I will get in trouble if I try to keep him grounded.

Gable continues to bond with the guys in the company. I held a social gathering for them last night in a private club and it couldn't have gone better. We ran into a friend from basic training and it was a gala reunion as he and Clark exchanged passionate memories of having served together back in the states. Apparently several other patrons in the club had enjoyed similar experiences because with very little provocation everyone was exchanging views and picking up their friendship just where they had left off. Clark and I had to leave before the event was over in order to make it back to the base, but you'll be able to read the memories on everybody's faces for the next few days.

I've made some observations that you might want to forward to Sam Marx in the Metro story department. When we make war films with "bomber crew" characters, we always seem to draw them from a broad assortment of backgrounds: Irish, Italian, Polish, Jewish, Southern, Rural, etc. Critics and sneak preview audiences have often complained that this was a contrivance. Believe it or not, it's actually how it happens in real life, except sometimes we have two people from the same background. The advantage of this is that guys from the same place can reminisce without bothering with backstory, and it creates a more immediate sense of bonding. Imagine having two Italians from New York talking about the festivals or the best neighborhood restaurants, or two Polish fellows from Milwaukee sticking up for their favorite wursthaus. Just a thought.

What would really be a good idea is if we could put some Negroes into the mix. I realize that the Army doesn't do this, but if we made the scenes so that they could be cut out when our pictures play in the Deep South, it would be a public service that could move us all forward.

I was just thinking that by the time you get this letter I will already have cabled you about Clark's status. Meanwhile could you let my folks in Brooklyn know that I'm alive and doing my bit? I'd write them myself but I think they'd appreciate hearing from you more than from me. They didn't exactly throw me a farewell bash when I moved to Hollywood. But you probably already know that thanks to Eddie Mannix.

Please give my regards to everyone at the studio. Tell them that the movies they send here for the servicemen and women to see are the best reminder of home that any of us could possibly have short of returning there alive, whole, and in a peaceful world.

More later,

Alan

I suppose the letter was more personal that it should have been, but I didn't care. I had to get it out of my system before the hangover arrived. Gable's talk about Ma made me think of my own mother. I thought I'd be too old to be homesick. I guess you never are.

Chapter 17

I FOOLISHLY FELL ASLEEP at the typewriter. Mavis did not knock me up at 0600 hours, nor at 0700 hours, nor at all. She was too busy taking charge of Captain Gable. At 0600, he walked into the briefing room at Peterborough all showered, shaved, and in uniform, looking just like a movie star. I figured that he could have checked in with me on the way and, seeing I had passed out, pulled me out of bed as he did before to join him. But then he knew what I would have done if he had.

About twenty desk-chair units were set up in the briefing room, which looked exactly like a classroom, except, instead of charts showing the Palmer method or human anatomy, there were maps. Maps of every place the Nazis occupied, which was most of Europe, Scandinavia, and Northern Africa. It was depressing; seeing the Occupation this way, Europe's future looked anything but guaranteed. It also made England stand out even more brilliantly as a tiny spec of freedom while the world was doomed under Hitler's booted foot.

Sitting in the chairs were perhaps twelve men, all of them flyers dressed in traditional well-worn leather jackets, and some sporting white scarves. If they had been chosen from Central Casting and costumed by Metro, it would not have been surprising. It was striking that these young men — none could have been more than twenty-five — wore such broken-in clothes. How broken-in must they have been inside? The British briefing officer, Captain Bramford, also appeared recruited from Central Casting. Pressed uniform, red hair with a center part and slicked back with Brilliantine, he actually carried a riding crop whose butt end he used to smooth his moustache — a moustache that seemed to grow from the middle out, rather than the top down. He didn't speak so much as announce. Come to think of it, he may well have been from Central Casting because at the back of the room were two 16mm cameras — one manned by Molina, the other by Battista — with Lewko on the sync audio recorder and Jeffers running around with the clapper and making script notes. There was no indication who was directing until Mavis stepped forward.

"All right, everyone, ignore the cameras and just go about your business. We want to make this look as authentic as we possibly can." She told the film crew, "Pay attention, since you'll be doing double duty."

Clark had been watching her, keeping out of it, but when she dared lecture his crew in such a flippant manner, he stepped up. "Miss Roberts, you are a civilian adjutant, are you not?"

"I am, Captain."

"And you understand that these men are in my unit."

"I do."

"And you certainly see me sitting here."

"I do."

"One of the things that Hollywood and the military have in common is protocol. On a set, if the director speaks to an extra, that extra gets bumped up to bit player and earns a higher fee because he has taken direction, as they call it. This is why, when a director wants to tell an extra to do a special piece of business, he has the assistant director do it. Are you following me on this, Miss Roberts?"

"I think I see where you're going, Captain." Gable had spoken evenly and calmly, but he was still Clark Gable. Mavis backed off.

Bramford ignored this. He was busy straightening his ascot and primping his moustache. If he'd had a mirror he would have looked into it. Jeffers stood beside him with the clapstick. "Don't be scared of the clap," he joked. Bramford ignored the obvious VD joke and said, "Listen, chap, I've flown home on the flak from Nazis guns trying to shoot me out of the sky. This toy of yours holds no interest."

Gable looked at the crew and they gave him signs that they were ready. "All right, everybody, settle please," he said. "Lights, please."

Jeffers flicked on the few lights that were mounted on the ceiling. Next, Gable called, "Roll camera!" Jeffers positioned the slate in front of Bramford. "Mission X, Take One, A and B Camera," he said, and made sure to slap the lined boards together extra loud in Bramford's face.

"Holy shit!" the officer said.

"Sorry about the flak, sir," Jeffers said innocently. "The mikes have to pick it up." He quickly ducked out of the way and Bramford began his spiel to the assembled flyers.

"The target for today is part reconnaissance and part defensive. Captain Nelson, this is a direct result of the mission you few last week. Care to hazard a guess?"

"Belgium," one of the flyers answered.

"Right you are," said Bramford. "Specifically?"

"Brussels?" said the young man next to him.

"Unless we want to give it a champ's try for Berlin," the first flyer joked.

"Stick to the playbook," Bramford said, realizing that his screen time would be cut short if he strayed. "The target for this afternoon is Antwep, Belgium. The resistance has told us that there is an ammunition storage facility that we can target with high accuracy if we do so during daylight hours. Of course, if we can see them —"

The whole room answered together, "— they can see us."

"Right you are," Bramford continued. "One hour there, one hour back. And all of you are coming back. Do you know why? Because you're only cleared to fly to the Belgian border. After that, the actual sortie is to be carried out a single plane piloted by Captain Nelson

All eyes turned to the quiet, expressionless young man seated at the rear of the briefing room. He did not wear a white scarf, though he did wear a crucifix. His blue eyes seemed incongruous set into such a young-looking face. This was Angier Nelson, the pilot of the B-17 that would carry the Little Hollywood Group, as well as its regular combat crew, over Nazi-occupied Antwerp. Seated below Nelson and his co-pilot was the bookish-looking navigator Hal Rudich. Confined in the plastic bubble ahead of them was the Mediterranean Lawrence Andriotti as bombardier, and behind him the navigator, pale-skinned Irishman Jimmy Langan. Compact Billy Murtaugh manned the ball turret. Aft were tail gunner and both waist gunners (sometimes called side gunners), the latter of whom stood exposed to the elements at openings in the sides of the aircraft.

They were all quiet because they knew that they were not turning back at the coast, It was their mission to continue to Antwerp, drop their payload on a Nazi an ammunition factory, take aerial photos of the damage and anything else the cloud cover permitted them to see, and then return to England. That was the plan, and that was the prayer.

The Little Hollywood Group was supposed to go along with cameras. And Gable was part of the Little Hollywood Group.

Bramford pulled down a map and traced the flight path. It was just like in a war movie. "The T-47 Thunderbolts will follow this corridor. Weather reports show a good tail wind so your ground speed will be 250 to 260 miles an hour. Unfortunately, the head wind also means that your return speed will be under 200. Ground temperature is warm: twenty-five Centigrade or about eighty Fahrenheit. When you reach this drop point to the Northeast, deploy your weapons, and turn about. The T-47s will rejoin you at the border and escort you home. Stay in radio contact for rendezvous. If the escort contingent does not hear from you, they will return alone. Are there any questions?"

Silence.

"All right, gentlemen, stations are at 0-8-30, engines at 0-900, and take-off by 0-9-30. Are there any questions?"

Nelson spoke for the room. "No, sir." He and Rudich rose, passed Gable and the "Little Hollywood Group," and glowered.

Gable said, "Cut." Lewko, Battista, Molina, and Jeffers started breaking down the equipment. "We're not gonna have a lot of time to get anything," he said. "Just shoot as much footage as you can and we'll sort it out later. Remember, whatever happens, keep rolling. Jeffers, stay on the pilot and be sure to get picture out the window so they'll know it's for real. Molina, focus on the bombardier. Battista, you can't record, but keep notes on what people say so we can wild them in later. I'll cover the gunner. Lewko, you know the rest."

"Yes, sir. Is this what they call a milk run?"

"Yeah," Gable said. "A milk shake."

The B-17G Flying Fortress was a majestic machine that captured the term for its own use. A four-engine heavy bomber, it was born in 1936 but evolved through ongoing changes at the Boeing Corporation until it reached its wartime homes with the U.S. Army Air Force and the RAF. Capable of staying aloft even with a fair amount of damage, it boldly flew daylight bombing missions, chiefly in the European theatre, although a few craft made their way to the Pacific toward the end of the war.

It was not the most maneuverable of planes but was unquestionably the most indefatigable. Of the entire crew, nobody was over twenty-five. Furnishings were Spartan to the extreme; nothing was upholstered, everything was metal, and at high altitudes you froze your ass off.

The crew to which Gable was assigned had named their craft "Eightball" and had it hand-painted on the fuselage. Everybody hoped it wouldn't live up to its name; macabre humor was a survival ploy.

Chapter 18

I SAT UP IN bed so fast that I flung myself onto the floor, then stood up so fast that I nearly passed out. My watch read eight o'clock — no time for that military time stuff — and I knew I was in deep haggis. I was still wearing last night's clothes — somehow I had pulled myself from the typewriter to the bed — so I quickly changed my shirt, pulled on my puke-stained shoes, and raced to the air strip.

On the way, I swore every curse word I knew. I figured I would be too late for the briefing, but I damn well intended to get to the plane and keep Gable from climbing aboard. I got there just as Clark and our group arrived at the bomber. I called out to him but he was focused on the aircraft as if it were his co-star. He circled it, touching its underside, feeling the rivets, and probing the Plexiglas on the nose gun canopy as if it was a religious relic. He looked like a country boy seeing his first city skyscraper as well as a sculptor getting the feel of a block of marble he was soon to carve. As he did, Captain Nelson neared him on his pre-flight inspection. Gable reached out his hand. "Clark Gable. Saw you in the briefing."

"Angier Nelson," the pilot remarked tersely.

"Thanks for letting us fly with you, Captain."

"'Tweren't my idea. Cuz of you and your crew, we're four bombs light."

Here is where I came in. "F'r'Chrissake, Clark what the hell are you doing?"

"Thought you were asleep, Junior."

Nelson, Murtaugh, Andriotti and the others paused from their routine to eat this up with a spoon.

"You are *not* flying," I said.

"That's not your decision, Lieutenant" Gable said, stressing *lieutenant*.

"Maybe not," I countered, "but it's my responsibility."

"I absolve you," said the King.

Remembering our adventure at the burning observation tower on the Florida beach, I said, "Then I'm coming along."

"Don't be an idiot."

"Try and stop me!"

If fools rush in where angels fear to tread, idiots lead with their chin and should know better. Without giving it a moment's thought, Clark hauled off and socked me out cold with such efficiency that I spun around into Lewko's ready catch. "Lock him in a closet somewhere and let's get out of here," he ordered.

While I was being dragged off, Molina asked Clark, "Sir, why do you keep calling him junior?"

"'Cause he's a junior publicist with the studio. They got him to enlist and protect me." Molina and the others laughed. Gable wanted in. "What's so funny?"

"Everybody thinks he's your orderly."

"Cut the crap," Nelson interrupted. "This baby's going to Antwerp. If you're riding with me, get your arse aboard."

The B-17 lumbered into takeoff position, its engines deafening and their vibrations rattling every inch of the craft. Elegant while standing still but ungainly when moving, the behemoth groaned as it awaited the take-off signal. Four massive propellers buzz-cut the late morning and pulled the huge machine forward until, at last, it turned to face the runway. It would take off first, followed by the T-47 escorts that flew more swiftly and would catch up with it almost immediately.

The moment it aligned with the runway, its crew focused their entire being onto the mission-at-hand. A wind sock near the tower showed Captain Nelson that there was a slight crosswind, and, as he guided the machine aloft, he expertly compensated for a perfect takeoff.

Four T-47s followed at one-minute intervals and suddenly they were a five-airplane sortie on a historic mission, historic because of their celebrity payload.

The noise raised me from unconsciousness but I found myself in darkness. A few slits of light played through the door and I realized that I had been placed in some kind of enclosure. The smell of disinfectant — not the odor one wants to deal with while nursing a hangover and a concussion — rose in my in my nose. Nausea quickly gave way to anger, then embarrassment that, faced with my first mission from Metro, I had failed.

For some god-awful reason, I thought of Sam Goldwyn's famous comment to his contract actor, David Niven — probably invented by his publicist — in response to Niven's request for a leave from filmmaking to join Britain in the war. Agreeing to put Niven on hiatus, Goldwyn supposedly said, "I'll cable Hitler and ask him to shoot around you."

The double-meaning only works if you know that the term "shoot around you" refers to finding other things to film while a particular actor is unavailable to appear on camera. I prayed that every possible meaning of that phrase would break in Clark's favor while he was on the Antwerp run.

Flying atop broken clouds at 20,000 feet, the fleet headed toward Belgium. Inside the Eightball, Lewko and Jeffers loaded their spring-driven cameras. No bulky studio cameras up here and no way to record sound. Just heavy metal combat cameras whose motors could run for thirty seconds at a time and had to be reloaded every six times. Battista made notes about the kinds of sounds heard in each section of the aircraft so they could reconstruct them later.

Molina hung on for the ride. Like most of the others he was not only seeing combat for the first time, it was his first plane ride. The B-17 was an unforgiving way to start. Passenger airliners were built with seats, padding, sound insulation, and windows small enough that, if you didn't want to see outside, you didn't have to. Military aircraft were metal, wood, glass, and noise. If you stood up, you clipped the top off your forehead. If you slipped, you fell into the bomb cache or out the side openings. Everything in a military plane said "exposed."

There were no loudspeakers, so each crew member heard the other, and broadcasts from other planes, through headphones built into their oxygen masks.

"Escort leader to fleet, Escort leader to fleet," the group commander on the lead T-47 said, "this is as far as we go. We'll catch you on the way back. Good luck and Godspeed."

The T-47s peeled off leaving the Eightball on its own. Nelson followed with his instructions.

"Okay, listen up," he said without emotion. "The escorts are away, so we're on our own. We are now over occupied Belgium, enemy territory. Let's stay on the ball."

Gable continued for the benefit of his team. "Now remember, I want close-ups. Faces. Hands. Molina, open the lens as wide as you can — f-two-point-eight — we can have the lab push it. Don't let the backlight blind you. Battista, are you keeping track of sounds?"

"What?" he said.

"Stop horsing around. You copy me?"

"Copy."

"Sir," Jeffers cut in. "Over here."

Jeffers said it to draw Gable to look at his camera, but Gable reached out and pushed Jeffers' camera to catch sight of Murtaugh entering the ball turret.

"He's the show, Jeffers, not me."

Nelson spoke again: "Pilot to bombardier. Arm your payload." Lewko focused on Andriotti.

"Aye-aye, sir," the young man said.

Murtaugh and Andriotti were like all the other combat men, only different. Young and exquisitely trained, they administered their skills with cold dedication. Murtaugh sat, vulnerable and silent, in the ball turret, ready to shoot in any direction at whatever might attack. Andriotti knew that, each time he pressed the release, he would rain death upon people, only a few of whom, at best, were the enemy. Although the aircraft could be fitted with extra bomb carriers for specific missions, its usual load was eight thousand pounds. They could be traded off for extra fuel for long runs or for additional passengers, as Gable's group was. As a result, the Eightball was only carrying four thousand pounds — still enough to do its job.

The crew's expertise was high or else they would not be on this mission. Yet their skill carried with it a profound curse, as it does to all men and women in war: whatever expertise they had in battle, it would be of little use in peace, yet they would carry the memory of having used it against their fellow man for the rest of their lives. Not that they would feel guilt; the event of war and the ritual depersonalization of the enemy would probably lift that burden from their psyches. No, it was becoming an expert at something that would be useless, even anti-social after cessation of hostilities. That places high on the list of ironies, if not the waste pile, of war.

I wonder if any of them thought about that while they were hyping themselves to fight.

Andriotti stood up and headed toward the bomb bay. "Where are you going?" asked Lewko, who was filming him.

"Follow me if you have the balls," Andriotti said. "I want to bless the bombs."

"Are you nuts or something?" Lewko asked, still rolling.

"Yeah," Andriotti said matter-of-factly. "You get superstitious. In case the weapons get lost on the way down, I want them to know where they're supposed to go. It's like a 'to-from' card on a Christmas present — if the recipient happens to be a Nazi. Comin' through." He pushed his way past the camera and lowered himself into bomb bay.

Gable made his way carefully to the opening above the ball turret where Murtaugh had taken his position. It looked worse seeing the boy in it than it had empty on the ground. One 50-caliber machine gun and one man. You had to be short to get in there, but no one on the flight looked taller than Murtaugh as he was manning it. There can be no more open, dangerous, or vulnerable position on a bomber, or a higher probability of combat death. As poet Randall Jarrell would write in his painfully evocative poem, "The Death of the Ball Turret Gunner," the station was like a womb, but instead of life, it birthed death. The poem (which would not be published until 1945) would only be five lines, but its imagery of being washed out of the ball with a hose would color the thinking of successive generations.

Perhaps Gable already had a handle on such thoughts as he asked, "What's your name, son?"

"Billy Murtaugh, sir."

"How old are you?"

"Nineteen, sir. Twenty next month. If I make it."

"Sure you will, son. I'll buy you a cake." He started to turn away but had to know more. "What's it feel like down there?"

"Like I'm jammed in the scrotum of a B-17."

"I mean, what's it feel like inside you?"

"If I thought too much about that, sir, I wouldn't be here."

How gracefully a nineteen-year-old tells a superior officer to mind his own business.

In the cockpit, Lewko was also getting his ass handed to him. "You wanna keep that thing out of my ear?" Nelson rebuked. The whirring of the spring-driven camera motor was loud enough to seep through the plane's rattle and hum.

"Sorry, sir," Lewko said.

"Why doncha point that at the ground? Look. Learn something.

See that smoke? That's factory smoke at a civilian target. That's off limits to us. Now see that clump of trees at nine o'clock?"

"Yes, sir," Lewko said, aiming the camera away.

Nelson was blunt. "That's a German observation post. If we're lucky, they haven't seen us yet."

"What if they have?"

"Then we can count on company, if not on the out, then on the way home."

Lewko was stoked. "Why don't we take them out now? I'll get it on camera."

"Negative," said the pilot over the engine noise. "We take out the primary as ordered. If they've seen us, it's too late, they've already radioed the Luftwaffe. If we have anything left to drop, which we won't, we'll get 'em on the return." Then Nelson made sure everyone on the plane heard him. "Okay, listen up. Primary target up ahead. Battle stations."

Clark Gable and Carole Lombard were married on March 29, 1939 and became celebrated as Hollywood's King and Queen. Her death on January 16, 1942 compelled him to enlist in the U.S. Army without caring whether he'd be killed.

Carole Lombard as she appeared in *My Man Godfrey*. When asked his choice of leading ladies, star William Powell suggested Carole, from whom he was divorced but whose talent he continued to respect. Their chemistry created an enduring screwball comedy. Credit: Studio publicity still

Gable and Lombard stand with Mrs. Elizabeth Knight Peters, Carole's mother. Peters and Lombard died in the plane crash. Mrs. Peters had a premonition of disaster but yielded to her daughter's desire to speed back to Los Angeles to be with Cark. The decision to take the plane instead of the train was decided by a coin toss.

Gable and Lombard on their ranch. Lombard was more of an indoor person but she loved Clark so much that she pretended to like the outdoors.

Lombard's friend Irene Dunne christens the Liberty Ship S. S. Carole Lombard on January 15, 1944, one day before the second anniversary of Lombard's death. Left to right: Gable, Mrs. Walter Lang (Madalynne Field; Lombard's secretary) and MGM chief Louis B. Mayer. Credit: Acme Telephoto.

The crew of the Eight Ball taken April 5, 1943 in England. A wind-blown Gable stands on the right.

The King of Hollywood becomes Private Clark Gable on August 12, 1942 as he is sworn into the U.S. Army by Col. Malcom P. Andruss in the Federal Building in Los Angeles.

Lt. Clark Gable walks past the tail gun of a B-17 as he prepares to fly a combat mission against the wishes of MGM. Photo dated June 12, 1943.

The visionary General Henry Harley "Hap" Arnold, the pioneer behind the creation of the U.S. Air Force, the RAND Corporation, and Pan-American Airways. It was ultimately his decision to ground Clark Gable.

The patch for the 351st Heavy Bombardment Group, nicknamed "Hatcher's Chickens" after their Commanding Officer, Major General Julian Hatcher.

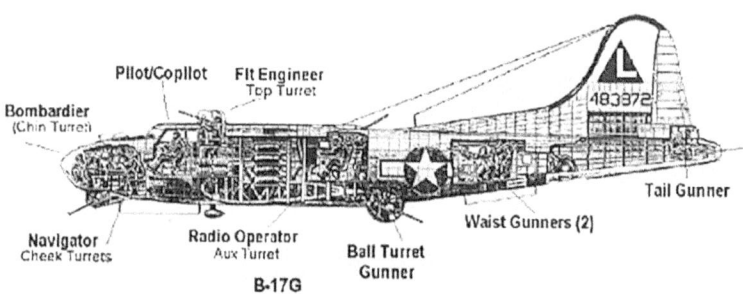

The stations of the B-17. Gable was most often a waist gunner on his five combat missions over occupied Europe.

Clark Gable poses in his B-17. He was embarrassed at so much attention when he believed other soldiers deserved it more, but he also knew that his presence in the Army was an effective recruitment incentive. Image courtesy of Fine Art America.

London's Dorchester Hotel as it appears today. During World War 2 it was on constant civil defense blackout alert. As the most posh place to stay in London, it was an oasis for visiting Hollywood types on studio expense account.

Lt. Col. James Stewart hangs out with Major Clark Gable in a photo taken in June 1943. Both men faced pressure over their celebrity status when all they wanted to do was fight the war. Photo credit: United States Army Air Force

Lionel Atwill, Jack Benny, and Carole Lombard in a scene from *To Be or Not to Be*, Ernst Lubitsch's supremely black comedy released in England in May 1942 and still showing throughout the war.

Clark Gable salutes on his promotion to Major.

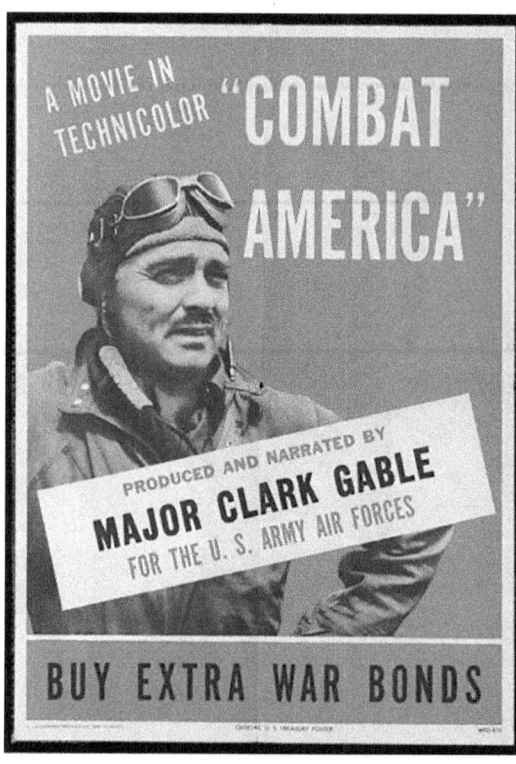

Poster for *Combat America,* the recruiting film Gable shot during his World War 2 service in England. It was designed as a recruitment tool but by the time it was finished the war was winding down and it was never widely shown.

Clark Gable speaks with a fellow officer in an interview segment from *Combat America.* Not surprisingly, Gable is totally at ease in front of even the perfunctory Signal Corps camera.

Poster for *Adventure*, Gable's first film on returning to MGM from the war. Famous for the tag line "Gable's Back and Garson's Got Him," it was an inauspicious return to the screen.

Gable and Marilyn Monroe co-starred in *The Misfits*. Monroe's lateness to the set and uncertain behavior led Gable to blow off steam performing his own stunts, generally believed to have led to his fatal heart on November 16, 1960

Chapter 19

THE EIGHTBALL, ALONE IN the late morning sky, droned boldly and unprotected on its way. The delayed start for the sortie was deliberate: the higher the sun in the sky, the better the reconnaissance photos. The bombing was almost secondary. The downside was obvious, and High Command had weighed the risks, particularly with Gable aboard. Yet the risk was believed to be lessened by the unusual plan of a single plane rather than a whole formation of B-17s. Perhaps it would confuse the Germans. And perhaps it would satisfy Gable that he had flown a mission and thereafter would be content to remain productively on the ground.

In the bomb bay, its doors poised to open, Andriotti was actually writing messages on the bombs. Each of them weighed at least a hundred pounds and could create unnumbered multiples of that in rubble when dropped. Knowing when to let them drop was his job, and he had practiced it on earlier runs. As he caressed his lethal weapons for deployment, he wrote on each of them, with a piece of chalk , "Adolf Sucks," adding hopeful insult to certain injury. "If you think this is nuts," he said when anybody asked him why he kept up this superstition, "ask any infantryman what his ritual is before he goes out on patrol."

"Target, twenty miles, mark," Nelson said. "Twenty miles, mark," confirmed Rudich. The crew sucked on oxygen through their masks. Not only couldn't the plane itself be pressurized — the waist gunners side openings made that impossible — it also couldn't be heated. Everyone on board fended for himself in the gale force of air that blew through the open stations. At eight degrees below zero and roughly half of the atmospheric pressure on the ground, this took a lot of fending. Any lower courted interception.

Soon it was time to go lower.

Andriotti returned to his post to find Molina looking through his bombsight. He pushed him aside roughly and didn't have to say why. This was the new Norden bombsight, ultimate top military secret. The Norden was a galactic improvement over the gut instincts of the bombardiers in previous generations. It was connected to the plane's auto-pilot and contained an early computer that calculated trajectory. In this way it could compensate for the myriad fluctuations in flight speed that could mean the difference between a bull's-eye and a wasted weapon. As the saying goes, "close" only counts in hand grenades and horse shoes. The Norden made "close" a thing of the past. It was so classified that bombardiers were under standing orders to destroy theirs if their plane got shot down. The Norden had to be kept out of the hands of the enemy.

Understanding this, Molina didn't take offense when Andriotti paid no further attention and simply informed Nelson, "Payload armed and ready, sir."

"Good work, kid," Nelson said over the intercom, "now let's give everybody a turn."

The massive aircraft banked and began descending — eighteen thousand feet, fifteen thousand feet, twelve. Ears popped; the crewmen dry-swallowed to equalize the pressure. The plane leveled at eight thousand and made for the primary target, the ammunition factory.

It was just north of the city of Antwerp but still close enough to spill over into civilian casualties. The Nazis built their factories near inhabited areas to discourage attacks by Allied bombers; they knew that the Allies would never risk the bad propaganda. What Berlin, in its arrogance, however, failed to grasp was that the people of occupied Europe would have eagerly given their lives to rid the earth of Nazi infestation. Nevertheless, the Allies made every effort to aim true (with the notable, strategic, and controversial exceptions of Dresden and Tokyo).

Nelson leveled at 5,000 feet. Cloud cover was light. Lewko poised with his camera. He almost forgot to roll film until he heard Andriotti say, "Bombs away!" The whirring of the camera mixed with the onrush of wind whistling through the open bomb bay doors as the compartment suddenly emptied itself of its deadly shells.

As the plunder of bombs fell to earth, the B-17 banked again, turning and climbing. Lewko was thrown off balance but managed to crawl to the window to shoot what he hoped were explosions on the ground a mile below. At least a dozen overlapping fireballs swallowed the Nazi ammunition depot. It was as if in a dream.

"Direct hit," Andriotti reported.

"Good work," commended Nelson, climbing to return to England. "Let's make like a baby and head out."

The G forces increased and Jeffers floundered. "I'm gonna lose it," he said.

"No you're not," Gable ordered, and aimed the young man away from himself.

"Aye aye, sir," Jeffers managed, coughing something up into his mouth and then swallowing it. He tried to smile in his embarrassment. "Hey, my ears cleared" and then, "I don't remember having hot dogs last night."

Gable looked around. No one on the plane was laughing. They were all watching the skies.

"Atta boy, Andriotti," Gable told the bombardier.

"Thank you, sir."

"Why's everybody so glum?"

"Because now comes the part we hate." It was Jimmy Langan, the navigator, who'd been silent throughout.

"What's that?" Lewko asked.

"Getting back alive."

It registered. Lewko asked, "What are the odds?"

"I dunno," Langan said with a straight face. "We've never made it before." It took Lewko a few seconds to realize he was being kidded.

Suddenly Murtaugh shouted, "Enemy aircraft, six-o'clock low."

The laughter stopped in a heartbeat. Nelson's calm voice set the tone: "Hold 'em off till the escort shows up."

Langan swallowed hard. He knew exactly how much distance they had to cover until that happened. He also knew there were no short cuts.

A single Focke-Wulf FW-190 was gaining on Eightball from behind. This was not hard to do; the single-seat fighter was built for speed and pursuit, and the Luftwaffe protected its air space with both. Captain Nelson lumbered the B-17 northwestward back toward England. The best he and his gunnery crew could hope to do was try and pick off the FW-190 as it buzzed back and forth on its strafing maneuver.

"He's coming back at us," Murtaugh shouted, and fired a burst. The tracers trailed into the sky and the enemy aircraft rolled and climbed to make another attack.

"Three o'clock high," said the waist gunner and let forth a volley. The Focke-Wulf returned it, strafing the plane and pulling up and out.

Bullets ripped through the fuselage. The sound of the perforations echoed around the metal shell. Rays of sun pierced the smoky interior through the cooling holes. One round whizzed past Gable's right ear as he was holding the hand-held camera against his eye. He flinched at the zip as it passed. The firing path brought the Focke-Wulf into full view of the starboard waist gunner who fired after it. No hit. The aircraft flew off into the mist and did not return.

"Just when we were getting ready to send him off," said Rudich, trying to sound sardonic.

"Everybody check in!" called Gable. "Roll call."

"That's my call," said Nelson.

"I don't give a damn whose it is," said Gable, "do it." One by one the voices responded into their microphones or into the still-tinged interior air.

"Lewko"

"Molina"

"Andriotti

"Jeffers"

"Battista"

"Lawson"

"Langan"

"Carpenter"

"Bosselman"

"Sparks."

"Muise."

"Rudich"

"Nelson"

There was silence. Gable, who had been counting on his fingers, shouted, "Murtaugh?" He scrambled to the ball turret and banged on the hatch. There was no answer.

"Murtaugh!" he shouted even louder.

He took hold of the handle on the hatch and pulled with everything he had. It did not give. "He's trapped in there!" he said, his voice edged with concern.

At once there was the sound of metal scraping as Murtaugh opened the door from the inside. Murtaugh picked cotton wadding out of his ears and looked around at everyone's relieved faces. "Are we having fun yet?" he said.

"Stations, everybody," Nelson said calmly into the intercom system. "Escorts returning ahead. We're going home."

Chapter 20

COLONEL HATCHER, MAVIS ROBERTS, and I stood with the ground crew in watching the Eightball land, taxi, and, it seemed, crawl to a stop. Each of us did so with escalating degrees of anxiety. When we finally saw its side looking like a connect-the-dots, our concern reached various levels of each of our throats. The ground crew placed blocks under its wheels as the door opened and the crew started tumbling out.

I'm afraid I acted like Fido eager to see his master return from work, or, worse, a young bride wondering if she was a war widow. "Where is he?" I said. "Where is he? Is he okay? Anybody hurt? What happened?"

"Steady, boy," said Mavis in a tone hardly calculated to help. "If he was injured, he would have been carried off first." Then she looked at me more closely. "Nice shiner," she said. I felt my eye and, sure enough, it was coming up.

The crew, and then our camera people, lined up and stood at attention. Clark and Captain Nelson were the last to deplane. They saluted Hatcher and took their places at command of the crew line awaiting inspection. Having the base commander greet an arriving flight was not only a novelty, it broke decorum; Hatcher was showing Clark the same kind of favoritism both Clark and the Army were trying to minimize, if not avoid.

"Clark? Clark, are you all right?" I said.

Hatcher looked daggers at me. So much for indulgence, "You're at attention, Mister," he barked. I stiffened.

Nelson saluted Hatcher. "All present with no injuries, sir. Mission accomplished."

"Very good work, all of you," Hatcher said. "The ammo factory you took out will slow the Nazis for weeks. I see you had a little trouble on the way back."

"Little is correct, sir," Clark said. "I guess the krauts didn't think we were important enough to send more than one plane. But he left his mark."

"What'd you think of your first combat mission, Captain?" Hatcher asked chummily.

"I admit it's a lot safer hanging in a model of a cockpit in front of a projection screen back at MGM," Clark said, "but I gotta admit, this really gets your blood going."

"He won't tell you, sir," Nelson said, acting nonchalant, "but if one of that Focke-Wulf's rounds had come through an inch closer, Rhett Butler would frankly have given a pretty big damn."

Gable brushed his ear. "I can still hear it," he smiled.

The image terrified me. "He's hurt!" I started screaming. "Can't you see he's hurt? Somebody get a medic!" I grabbed Gable's arm and started to lead him ahead of the others to the infirmary.

"Get your hands offa me," he said, pulling away. Then he stumbled and almost fell to the ground. He righted himself immediately, but we all looked down at the same time.

His combat boot had the heel shot off.

"Sonofabitch," he said. "I thought I felt something knock me in the foot. I figured it was just the plane bouncing."

"You almost lost your foot *and* your ear?" I gasped, by now frantic. "I gotta get to a teletype. I gotta let the studio know. I can see the headline: 'King Dodges Death'"

Gable took me by the collar with his left hand and drew his right hand back into a fist. "You want a matched set?" he said. I flinched for the sake of my good eye.

"I guess we can hold off a little while telling the press," I said.

Gable glared at me and told Hatcher, "If you'll excuse me, Colonel, I'd like to have a few words with my orderly."

Hatcher said sternly, "Have as many as you want" as Clark yanked me aside.

"Are you trying to make me a laughingstock?" he growled.

"I promised Mr. Mayer I'd keep you safe."

"If L.B.'s so worried about me, tell him to loan out Hitler to RKO and nobody will ever see him again."

"Are you trying to get yourself killed?" I said.

Clark took exception. "You're out of order, orderly," he said.

"Captain Gable," Hatcher called. "Front and center!"

Gable pushed me aside and marched confidently to where the crew had assembled. Mavis was rearranging them — featuring Clark and Hatcher, naturally — as her photographer took picture after picture.

"Another one, please. That's right, shake hands. Now hand on shoulder. Clark, point to your ear. Now point down to your heel. All right, Colonel, now you point to Clark's heel." And on it went.

A reporter pushed through and got Gable's attention. "Pardon me, sir," he said, "Colin Murray of the *Times*. I'd like a comment, sir. Fieldmarshall General Goering of the Luftwaffe has announced a fifty thousand reichmark bounty on your head. There's also a promotion and an extended vacation to whomever shoots you down or captures you and brings you to Berlin. What answer would you like to send him?"

Clark weighed his words for a moment and said, "You can tell Goering and Adolf and Dr. Goebbles and the other Nazi scum that I'm under exclusive contract to Uncle Sam. Nobody's gonna parade me around in some monkey cage. And furthermore —" I couldn't hear what else he said over the applause and cheers. When it died down, Hatcher said, once more, "Congratulations, men. And to you, too, Captain Gable. You got your wings today. Now fall out for de-briefing in one hour."

A round of salutes and the men headed for the briefing room. They surrounded Gable, slapped him on the back, mussed his hair, and treated him like one of their own. What a pub full of beers and a staged bar fight failed to pull off, a Luftwaffe bullet had accomplished it in spades.

Mavis sidled over to me. "Well, Alan," she said, "it looks as if your client not only got his wings, he's finally been promoted to the rank of human being."

I may not have heard the rest of Clark's quote, but Mr. Mayer and Howard Strickling read it in the *Times*.

"'And furthermore,'" Strickling recited while Mayer fumed, "'if I get shot down, I'm not bailing out, I'll put an end to it myself.'"

"Put an end to it himself?" Mayer fulminated. "I have money in that son of a bitch! He can't kill himself till his option's up."

"He means he'll kill himself if he's shot down. He doesn't want to be a POW."

"Where's that damn kid?" Mayer charged. "The one you said — the one you *promised* — would keep Clark's ass on the ground."

"He was unconscious," Strickling said, referring to my terse private report of the incident. "When he tried to stop Clark from going up, he punched out his lights."

"Punched him?" Mayer sounded worried. "Did Clark hurt his hand?"

Strickling went back to reading from the *Times*. "When asked by reporters if he'd had his fill of combat, Gable smiled and said, quote, 'Are you kidding? I'm just getting a taste for it.'"

Mayer steadied himself on the edge of his desk, grabbed the rim as he felt his way around it dramatically, and sat down heavily in his leather chair. "I'm having a heart condition. I'm seeing my life flash in front of me. It isn't even over yet and it needs reshoots." Strickling did nothing; Mayer's spells passed as soon as he realized his audience was on to him, as Strickling routinely was. "Okay, okay," the mogul said, getting a grip. "Tell the kid I'm letting him off the hook this time. Now that Gable's made one flight, it better be out of his system. We don't want him dead, Hatcher doesn't want him dead, millions of moviegoers don't want him dead. Only Clark wants himself dead. We outnumber him. This is still a democracy, right?"

"I'll tell him," muttered Strickling, figuring that Mayer would never remember what he actually said, only what he was thinking, and that didn't make any sense, either.

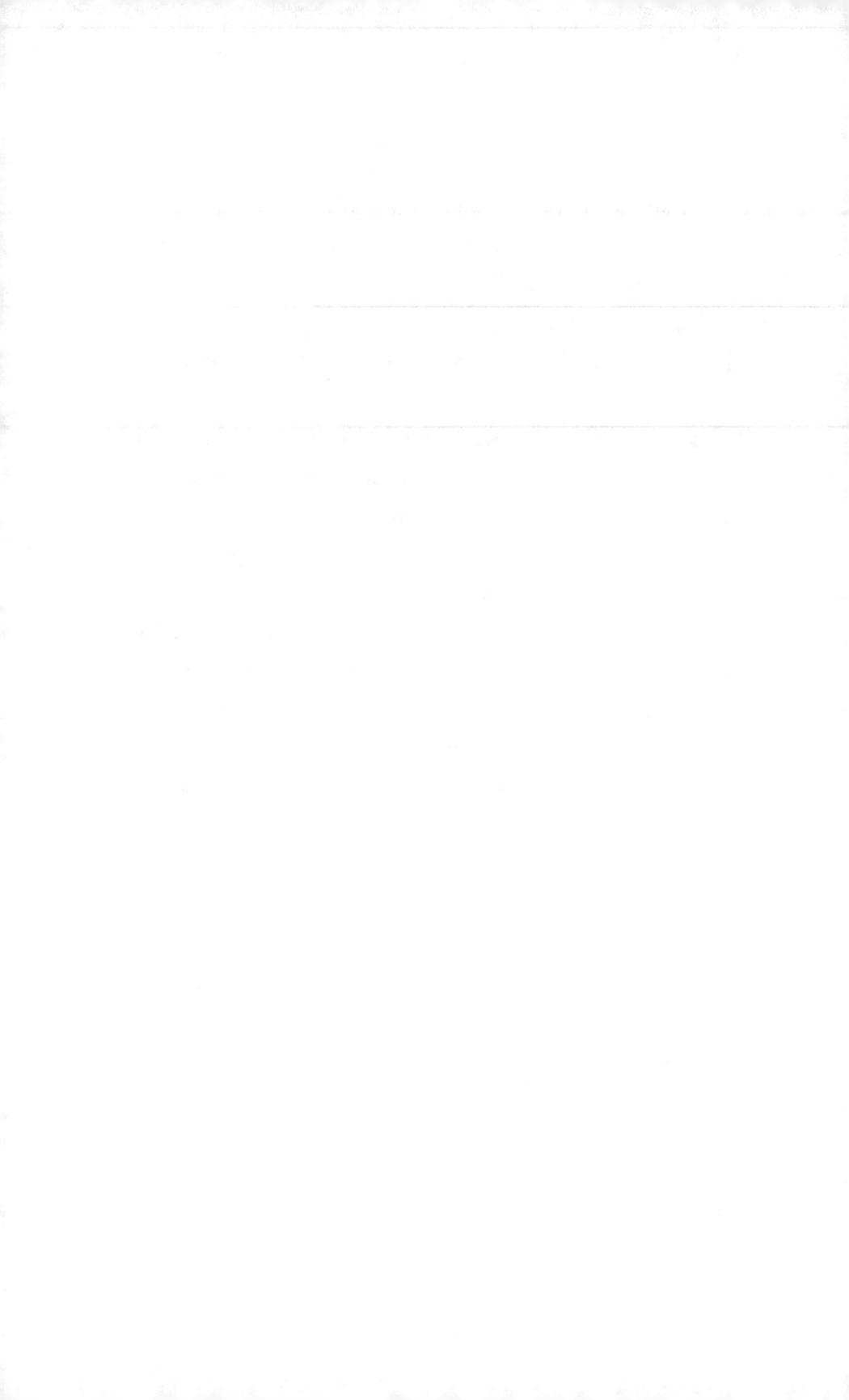

Chapter 21

"SON OF A BITCH, Clark, you make it sound like you've got a death wish!" I couldn't help repeating myself. My left eye had been swollen shut with a perfect right cross from the King of Hollywood, and it was my job to take him to task, even if I had to squint to do it. "If you die, nobody wins."

He was having none of it. "There's five million men and women fighting for freedom," he said emphatically. "I don't call their dedication a death wish. I call it patriotism. At the very least, I'm doing my duty."

"Oh, save the speeches for the newsreels," I said. "You've made your point. You flew. You got shot at. Why risk your luck again? Please, please, finish this war on the ground."

We were on our way to Hatcher's office to send a cable to MGM. Clark and I agreed that it would be newsy but noncommittal, but that's as far as he would go along with me. Whatever we sent would be given a cursory look-at by the base censors, then sent on to headquarters where more sophisticated examiners would search it for secret codes or suspicious words.

Even though we had stopped walking at the door of Hatcher's office, I didn't go in. I wanted an answer from Clark, and he wasn't about to give me one. "Haven't you got a cable to send?" he said, and his concentration was over. I entered the outside office unfolding a handwritten draft I'd brought along while Clark stayed outside getting some sun. I could see him through the window.

Mavis was already at the Telex attending to other reports. "Good morning, Miss Roberts," I tested the waters before asking how long she'd be. "Or should I call you 'Adjutant Roberts'? I suppose 'Mavis' is out of the question."

She didn't bother to look up. "Just a moment,' said in that semi-there way a kid tells his mother, "yes, I heard you" when she tells him she's going to the store while he's reading comic books, and then five minutes later your kid brother comes in and asks, "where'd mom go?" and you honestly don't remember.

Mavis was a whiz at the keyboard. I wondered if I could get her to type my cable for me, then thought better for a lot of reasons. I killed time by looking at the framed photos on the wall, my back to her, but focusing on her reflection in the picture glass. I wanted to catch her sneaking a glance at me. She didn't.

In publicity we have a name for photographs where two people shake hands like old friends and smile for the camera. We call them "grip and grin" shots. Sometimes they involve handing over a check to charity, receiving an award plaque, or just a posed shot for the public relations of it. The first shot the photographer takes is usually the best. If you ask for more than one, the people doing the gripping and the grinning start to feel like idiots. Hatcher seemed to have a fetish about grip-and-grins. According to his wall, he had met every celebrity, world leader, politician, or local businessman that walked within a shutter's distance of the base. Some were even autographed, which means he sent them to the person who sent them back signed. But what jumped out at me was that Hatcher looked exactly the same in each picture. He had a fixed smile and a fixed stance, always on camera right, and looked not so much like hail-fellow-well-met as a life-sized Hatcher cutout that tourists posed with because the real thing was busy.

I don't mean to criticize Hatcher for being a tireless self-promoter. I'm just saying that he looked like one. You could probably stack up all the photos and run them through your fingers like a Disney flip book and Hatcher would look like he was standing still while the people at the other end of his handshake would change. It took Mavis's words to break my reverie.

"Now, then, what is it?"

Okay, the next part will take some explaining. When Mavis turned around, the light coming in the window hit the back of her head and created a kind of glow. Not a halo, but a glow. The room light bounced off the newsprint on the desk and reflected up at her face in a warm, earthy softness. Her hazel eyes were clear and moist as they looked at the paper I carried in my hand and then up to my own eyes. She was both intimate and remote, even beautiful in a "yes-but-she-still-hates-me" kind of way. Why hadn't I noticed this before, and now what am I going to do about it? I stood in silence and stillness.

"Let's have a look, then." Mavis, seeing me gob-smacked, gently took the paper from my hand and read it. "Has this been censored?" she asked.

I think I shook my head No, but I don't remember. Ignoring me, Mavis read my message back to me. "To Howard Strickling, Metro-Goldwyn-Mayer Studios, Culver City, California. Our heroic friend is unharmed, repeat, unharmed," she read. "You don't need to repeat it, Alan; they'll be holding the message in their hands."

I felt like my writing was being corrected in front of the whole class by Mrs. Henderson, my tenth grade English teacher.

"He says," Mavis continued reading, "that after making pictures with Bill Wellman, World War Two is a snap." She raised her right eyebrow and looked up again. "That's a bit cheeky, isn't it?"

She must have seen something in my face, because she moved her swivel chair across the room, still sitting in it. God help me, I followed her around the office like a puppy. "Give Clark's regards to Hedda and Louella, and he says to make sure you're sending the money you promised to Otto's widow." And to me, she said, "that's so sweet."

"You'll be happy to learn that Colonel Hatcher has issued orders grounding Clark for the duration of the war," she went on reading. "Has he?" she asked, and shook her head dismissively. By now we were both across the room near the water bubbler. I blocked her way so neither she nor her chair could pass. "Really, now," she said sharply, "you know that the Colonel has done nothing of the kind."

"I know," I agreed, "but why worry them? Sign it Greenberg and call me Alan."

Although I didn't want to take my eyes off of Mavis, I noticed out of the corner of them that Clark was watching us through the window. He wasn't even being casual about it, either, he was pressing his nose against the glass and cupping his hands around his eyes to get a better look.

"I can't lie about orders," Mavis huffed, shifting to the right.

"I thought you wanted us to get along," I countered, blocking her move.

"We'd get along better if you didn't put words in the Colonel's mouth."

"I bet we'd get along better if you put food in your mouth."

"What on earth do you mean by that?" she said, allowing me to step behind her, forcing her to rotate toward me.

"It's a dinner invitation. I'm sure we can find a place that serves actual food instead of Woolton pie or carrot loaf with sawdust stuffing."

I finally got a smile out of her as she turned back to the Telex and began typing. Not looking at me, she said, "At least you didn't offer me chocolates and stockings."

"Can't I see you off base?" I asked.

"You're pretty far off base now," she shot back. "Will there be anything further?"

"Can I watch you type?"

"You *can*," she said, summoning a schoolmarm attitude. "The question is whether you *may*."

"Save your semantics," I said, leaving without looking back at her. "Cheerio."

The door hadn't even shut behind me when Clark took his hand and slid it downward at an angle while whistling — the international symbol among guys for crashing like a plane.

"She hates me," I said. Gable shook his head.

"How can a guy who filled casting couches for other people at the studio strike out on his own time?"

This blind-sided me. "What are you talking about?"

"Come on, Junior, it's no secret that you were in charge lining up a private evening's entertainment for producers, theatre owners, politicians, and anybody else the studio needed on their side."

"Hey, I'm just a publicist," I protested. "Why do people always think the worst of publicity. After all, we're the world's oldest profession."

"No you're not," Clark said. "The girls you procured were the world's oldest profession."

"No," I corrected. "They're the world's *second* oldest profession. The publicist is. Because before the first hooker went into business, some poor publicist had to get out a press release on her."

Clark laughed. "All it takes is persistence, Junior."

"Sometimes yes, sometimes no," I equivocated. "Lemme give you a f'r'instance. You know how it is when you meet a girl and you want her to go out with you, and you ask her and she says no?"

Clark had to think about it before answering, "No."

"You've never been turned down by a girl?"

"Um, no."

"Let me show you something, Clark," I said, trying another tack. I turned him to face our reflections on the window. "What do you see?"

"A guy with big ears, a stupid nose, and false teeth," Gable said. "And he's standing next to a guy who doesn't give himself enough credit."

"You know what I see?" I said. "I see a plain-looking short guy standing next to Rhett Butler, Fletcher Christian, and all the heroes who ever got the girl in every movie you ever made."

Before he could respond, Mavis's reflection appeared behind ours and we both wheeled about to face her.

"And they say women spend hours in front of the mirror." She said, and handed me a piece of newsprint with typing on it. "Here's your confirmation of delivery and your original returned."

Clark broke the awkwardness. "Tell me something, Miss Roberts, when you look in this window, what do you see?"

She faced the glass. We all did. When I looked at Clark, I saw him looking at her. When I looked at her, I saw her looking at Clark. Then they both realized what was happening and they quickly looked at me, but it was too late.

"I'll tell you exactly what I see," she said. "I see I'll have to tell the duty sergeant to have someone clean this filthy window." Clark and I both laughed. It was nervous laughter, but it was laughter. "Was I being funny?" Mavis said.

"No, Miss Roberts," Gable chuckled, "you were being sensible. Perfectly sensible."

Mavis turned from the window and faced me. "I've been thinking about your dinner offer, lieutenant. Perhaps you and the Captain would like to take my friend Elizabeth and me on one of those, oh, what do you Americans call them?"

Clark and I answered in unison: "A double-date."

"Yes!" Mavis said, expressing measurable enthusiasm. "That would be super!"

"If we can hitch a ride into London, maybe we can catch a play," I suggested, my mind already working on who I could hit-up for comps.

Mavis nodded in agreement. "If you can work it out for this weekend, let me know. Fair enough, lieutenant?"

"Alan," I corrected.

She turned to Clark. "Fair enough, Captain?"

"Clark," he corrected.

"Super!" she repeated. "I'll tell Elizabeth!"

We watched her walk back into Hatcher's office. "What just happened?" I asked Clark.

"We're gonna get laid!"

"That's easy for you to say," I moped.

"Where's your self-confidence, Junior?" he said as buoyant as I'd ever heard him. He took his hand, made it into an airplane as before, but this time aimed it toward the sky and walked away whistling.

I looked again at my reflection in the window. A thought crossed my mind. Going on a double date is risky enough, but how do you make time with a girl when your competition, sitting at the same table, is Clark Gable?

Chapter 22

LONDON CRUMBLED DURING THE war; Londoners did not. The English resistance to change, often misconstrued as blind adherence to tradition, displayed itself in a remarkable refusal to allow the war to alter the Empire. Of course it did anyway, though not as profoundly as had the first world war. "The Great War," that catastrophe that dragged all of Europe into a pit of death and destruction — like one climber jumping off a mountain and pulling the others along — led to the loss of an entire generation, the effect of which was the rupture of family dynasties and a reshuffling of labor, clergy, and leadership over the twenty years that followed.

Hitler's blitzkrieg against England from September of 1940 to May of 1941 did not achieve the Nazi's goal; rather than break England's spirit, it solidified its patriotism. Nevertheless, by our arrival in 1943, there were some concessions to deal with. Nightly blackouts, for example, dimmed the electric fires of Piccadilly Circus to those that were minimally required: the Underground, stoplights, and the discrete "open" signs that stalwartly marked business as usual. Theatres, of course, thrived, although it was not uncommon to have performances interrupted by air raid sirens and, occasionally, audience evacuation to the tube (subway) stations that served as shelters. Sometimes the performers would even continue the show underground.

Christopher Wren's exquisite Cathedral of St. James was destroyed, as were the Shaftsbury Theatre and Queen's Theatre. The number of small businesses and homes that fell to bombing and fires is inestimable. The classic photograph of St. Paul's Cathedral standing defiantly amid the smoke and fires surrounding it is as much a symbol of emotional England as of physical England.

Motor traffic in the city was profoundly changed. Individual automobiles yielded to service vehicles and omnibuses. Horse drawn carts and carriages returned. With so many men in uniform, women took over jobs there as in the States.

Food rationing was a constant challenge. Housewives learned to fabricate healthful, if not always tasty, meals from whatever ingredients were available and permitted. Cabbages and potatoes became more than staples, they were easy to grow and omnipresent. Victory gardens flourished. Fish, though not rationed, was hard to get, so tins (cans) of anchovies mixed with starchy vegetables gave the impression of seafood. In the cities, eggs were powdered, butter was scarce, and meat even more so. Restaurants and hotels fell under a different rationing system but they still had to follow the law, and this meant that, when Clark and I took Mavis and Elizabeth to supper, we had to make sure it was a place that could actually produce a meal.

We decided to dine at the Dorchester on Park Lane, east of Hyde Park, a hotel known not only for its elegance and cuisine but as one of the most soundly constructed buildings in London. I girded for the expense (as publicist I would be responsible) and hoped that the studio would cover the tab. As it turned out, the Dorchester is where Mr. Mayer and the other top executives stayed whenever they visited London, so Metro was known to the management and all I had to do was flash my employee identification.

Elizabeth Manning, Mavis's friend, worked in the City of London (which, I was surprised to learn, is a corporate entity separate from, but located physically within, metropolitan London). Mavis and I waited in the lobby for her to join us. I tried not to be obvious staring at the Dorchester's magnificent furnishings which dated from its opening in 1931. Given that 1931 was when the world had been thrown into a Great Depression, the opulence surrounding us was obscene as well as tasteful. When Mavis caught my jaw dropping at the decor, she read my mind.

"Yes, you can hardly tell there's a war on."

"Or that there was a Depression."

"For some people, there was no Depression," she remarked.

"That's what I like about London."

"You've been here before?"

"No," I fudged, "I was trying to sound worldly and endearing." My honesty won me a genuine smile.

"And you did," Mavis said winningly. I waited for more, but none came.

"Is your friend coming soon?"

"From work. She didn't know whether she'd take the tube or walk. The blackout goes into effect at sundown." Then, coyly, "What about your friend?"

"He's looking for newspapers."

Mavis looked perplexed. "There's a boy selling them outside if there are none in here."

"I mean reporters. Avoiding them. He's freshening up in the gents — is that right, "the gents"?

"Yes, and it's also called the loo."

"He'll be right along."

"Are you trying to sound British?" Mavis asked. The smile was back and she was standing slightly closer than usual. Not enough to get hopeful over, but, you know, closer. I was about to narrow the gap when Mavis's gaze was drawn toward the main doors. "Ah, here's Elizabeth."

A gorgeous blonde woman in a tastefully revealing dress glided over to us. "Elizabeth Manning," Mavis continued, "may I present Lieutenant Alan Greenberg?"

I didn't know whether to shake her hand or kiss it. I went with shake. "How do you do?"

"Fine, thank you, and you?" she said, mesmerizingly.

All three of us were at a loss for words. Then Mavis said, "Elizabeth is my flat-mate."

"Flat?" I said, trying not to look at Elizabeth's cleavage.

"You call them apartments," Mavis reminded me.

"Yes, I moved in six months ago after Gerry took mine," Elizabeth said.

"Your boyfriend took your flat?" I asked.

"The Germans," Elizabeth said as though she was talking to a complete idiot, which her appearance had made me. "We call them Gerry. They bombed it."

"'Gerry,' I like that," I said. "Our names for them are more disgusting." Fortunately, I couldn't think of any, then I saw my salvation as Clark approached us from across the lobby. "Miss Manning, now it's my turn to make introductions. I'd like you to meet my friend. May I present —"

I didn't have to. Gable's power preceded him. I'd never seen him so completely done up. At Metro he was either in his character's costume or casual clothes getting ready to put on his character's costume. Tonight he was dressed to the nines and beyond. He was wearing civvies, of course, but his civvies came from Saville Row. Every head in the lobby turned toward him. He glided across the thick-pile carpet as if he wasn't even touching it. He knew where each foot was going to land before he brought it down. When he got near, he smiled at Elizabeth and offered his hand.

"How do you do, Miss Manning? I've been looking forward to meeting you all week. I'm so glad you could join us." He greeted Mavis with similar cordiality, nodded to me, and we walked as a foursome to The Grill.

"Four for dinner," I said to the Maitre D' in my most "arrived" manner. "The reservation is under Greenberg."

The Maitre D', properly outfitted in full tux with center-parted hair and pince-nez spectacles, acted as though he had memorized the evening's roster because he answered without even looking at his book, "I'm sorry, Mr. Greenbaum, we don't seem to have your name and we're entirely booked for both seatings this evening."

"The name is Greenberg," I said, carefully acting stuffy instead of snotty. "I called two days ago and then re-confirmed this morning."

This time the man deigned to look at his book. "I'm afraid there must be some mistake, sir, because we don't have anybody named Green-anything. Perhaps you and your party would be more comfortable at the Spatissereie across the lobby."

"All right," I said. "I get it. I didn't think this happened at the Dorchester, but —" and I reached for my wallet.

"Just a moment," Clark stepped forward. He had kept out of view until now for reasons that must have played out for him a hundred times. "Perhaps you inadvertently listed it under the wrong name. Try G-A-B-L-E."

The Maitre D's pince-nez flew off his nose. "Of course! This way, sir," he said, trying not to appear as flustered as he was. He walked us through the grand dining room. Conversation stopped. Forks dropped. It was as if the English King, not the Hollywood King, had arrived. We were ceremoniously seated at the most visible table in the middle of the room, each of us handed menus by a personal waiter, and tried not to feel two hundred eyes checking us out.

"Everyone is staring at us," Elizabeth said in a stage whisper.

"Yes, Madame," said the Maitre D.

"Is there a more private table?" she asked.

The Maitre D' had regained his aplomb. "If Madame doesn't mind, one learns that it's better to seat celebrities in full view so that everyone in the room can easily see them rather than have each diner contrive to walk past the table on the way to the powder room and make an endless stream of interruptions." He left us alone. Elizabeth, Mavis, and I tried not to feel stared-at. Clark was used to it, of course.

"Just be careful picking your nose," he said.

Chapter 23

IT WASN'T THE BEING stared at by our fellow diners that bothered me during dinner, it was never being left alone by the serving staff. I'd been with my share of celebrities — junior publicists are always being tapped to accompany and run interference for contract players at personal appearances — but to suddenly find myself having so much glitter scattered at my own place setting was a novelty, and not a pleasant one. Clark's wisecrack about not picking our noses was on target; I was afraid to smear margarine (no butter) on my bread lest I accidentally drop a crumb and have six white-jacketed busboys scramble to clean it up.

I knew manners. Not that I was raised with them; if you held your pinky out in my Brooklyn neighborhood, somebody would cut it off. But Metro, like the other studios, maintained a squad of teachers who put all their contract people and their support staff through rigorous training in how to stand, how to dress, how to speak, how to be interviewed, and which fork to use. All of this to polish the stars while the moguls themselves practically fed out of a trough.

As one who might be called upon to escort the stars or deal with the press, I was included in many of these lessons. I must say that I'm rather proud of what I learned, and I made it a point to use it at the Dorchester. I steadied Mavis's chair as she sat, rose when she rose, offered her the bread first, spoke equally with her and with Elizabeth, and I remembered that the napkin goes in the lap, not tucked into the collar. I knew which was the fish knife, the salad fork, and not to drink the finger bowl. I let Clark order the wine but I knew to cover my glass if I declined to drink (one of us had to stay sober, and I was hoping it wouldn't be Mavis).

The formality reminded me of a story that was sworn to me as true. Screenwriter Herman Mankiewicz, who was both a great wit and a great drunk (he co-wrote *Citizen Kane* for RKO), was dining at producer Arthur Hornblow's home. The aptly named Hornblow was a renowned host, taking pride in using the finest china, having the best silver, and serving the most perfect meals. Halfway through dinner, Mankiewicz, who was gloriously inebriated, suddenly vomited at his place setting. A terrible hush fell over the room but it was broken by Mankiewicz himself who not only put himself down but needled his pretentious host by saying, "Don't worry, Arthur, the white wine came up with the fish."

Clark and Mavis ignored the swarm of waiters, sommeliers, and busboys that orbited around us, but Elizabeth and I became fascinated. Rolls, crudités, and replacement utensils appeared from nowhere. The moment we took a sip of water, our glasses were refilled. No one ever had to touch the wine bottle. At the end of every course, each plate was lifted and replaced with the next one in perfect unison. Everyone wore gloves and the most nondescript facial expressions I had seen since walking out of a studio screening of *The Vanishing Virginian*.

"We didn't order all this," I whispered to Clark.

"Just ignore them," he whispered back.

Elizabeth shared my concern. "Don't we need a ration book?" she asked.

"Ignore them," Gable repeated.

"They're making such a fuss!" Elizabeth said.

"*Ignore them!*"

"How?" I said, "they're practically chewing my food for me." At that moment, the Grill's string quartet struck up a waltz.

"Here's how," Clark said, offering his hand to Mavis. "May I have this dance?" Mavis's look let me know that she was as surprised by this as I was, but I dutifully rose as she got up. As he helped her to rise, Clark leaned down to me and said, "Why don't you two kids get acquainted?" leaving Elizabeth and me alone at the table.

Both of us were stunned and tried to start a conversation. Instead, we buttered (margarined) our bread. Finally I took the plunge.

"So," I asked Elizabeth, "the Germans bombed your house. We got back at them the other day."

The band, as they say, played on, and I could see Clark and Mavis enjoying their dance. Meanwhile, my nervous comment had opened Elizabeth's conversational floodgate.

"That's what most people think," she said as I tore my attention away from Mavis and Clark, continuing a conversation I didn't recall our having begun. "Folding bandages is an exacting job. First you take the outer edge and align it against the center, being careful not to overlap. It has to unfold easily with a single hand movement because ones other hand is usually holding forceps, a sponge, or even a sterile swab." She must have seen me glancing again at Mavis and Clark because she asked, "Am I boring you, Alan?"

I ached to say Yes. Instead, I said, "How could hospital work be boring? After all — "

That was her cue to pick up where she had left off. "And that's just the bandage-wrapping part. Sterile compresses require even more precise skills."

Suddenly I was saved by the Luftwaffe. The lights dimmed, sirens went off, the music stopped, and the Maitre D' started blowing a police whistle.

"Goodness," Elizabeth shrieked, "it's an air raid!"

Around the perimeter of the restaurant, waiters made sure that the blackout drapes were fastened. Flambé fires were covered and candles on the table were immediately extinguished. Torches were produced rather than risk flames.

"Ladies and gentlemen, this is a readiness drill. I have been informed that there are no enemy planes in sight. The civil defense ministry wants us to conduct these drills as a matter of safety. We shall not need to clear the room, but please gather your personal things to avoid forgetting any of them in the dark. Once again, please, this is only a drill."

All right, so the Luftwaffe had nothing to do with it. But by the time everyone in the restaurant had finished crossing themselves, checking their purses and wallets, chugging their wine, and collecting their thoughts, Mavis and Clark had disappeared.

The lights were just coming back up when Elizabeth finally noticed that we were alone. "Somebody must have pulled a switch," she said.

"What do you mean?"

"When Mavis asked me to come along tonight, she said I might like your friend, but she didn't tell me his name. I pressed her and pressed her and she finally told me who it was. What a surprise that I was being set up with Clark Gable! How do you think I felt when he went after her?"

I wanted to say the same thing, but decency (and, let's face it, a wallow in self-pity) prevailed, so I agreed, "Yes, this evening is full of surprises."

"Indeed," Elizabeth said. "It reminds me of the time I was doing hospital volunteer work and our supervisor told us to switch suppositories instead of what she really meant, which was to exchange them."

Gable and Mavis returned to the dining room a few minutes later. By then, Elizabeth had worked her way up from suppositories to tongue depressors. As the saying goes, "Ask me no questions and I'll tell you no lies," but both Elizabeth and I were burning for Clark and Mavis to voluntarily tell us where they had been for the last ten minutes. They did not, so we finished dinner, sipped our tea in uncomfortable silence, and let me pay the check. Not surprisingly, the Maitre D' who had lost my reservation had no trouble allowing me to sign the dinner to the studio's account.

When Gable and I dropped Mavis and Elizabeth at their flat and said our chaste goodnights, I politely thanked Elizabeth for her company. "I've had an exciting night," she said enthusiastically. "Super, in fact."

"Me too," I lied. "It's the closest I've come to playing doctor since I was twelve."

"When Mavis said she had a famous friend, I hardly imagined!"

"Oh, I'm not that famous," I said, pushing a pebble around with the toe of my shoe.

"I meant Clark."

"Oh," I said, trying to sound hurt. "That's me, always the hero's best friend."

By now all four of us were in the first floor hall. The ladies' flat was upstairs.

"Thank you so much, Clark," Mavis said softly. "I had a super time."

The pause was so pregnant that it just about gave birth: would Gable kiss Mavis goodnight?

Instead, he shook her hand, said, "See you at the office," then shook Elizabeth's hand, and said, "The cab's waiting." I decided against kissing anybody and followed him out the door.

Mavis and Elizabeth stood together in the vestibule wondering what had happened.

The taxi ride back to the base was an adventure in awkwardness. I led with, "I thought we were friends."

"I gave you Elizabeth," Clark said. "She's a knockout."

"Only in the sense of being unconscious," I returned. "She was supposed to be yours."

Gable took a moment to process something, then turned to me in all earnestness. "I like 'em homely," he said in a low voice so the cabbie wouldn't hear.

I stared at the meter. "Mavis is not homely."

Gable shifted uneasily. "I'm not saying her face would stop Big Ben, but — see, if a pretty girl says she went out on a date with Clark Gable, it would be all over town. But if a plain-looking girl ever says she dated me, nobody would believe her." He let that settle in, then added, "Sometimes it's easier to talk to a woman, even if you don't try to score."

"What was your plan with Mavis?" I asked, rather boldly, I thought.

"She's the Colonel's adjutant," Gable said. He looked at me. As he did, a thought entered his brain that I assumed had been there all along, but it hadn't been.

"Good lord," he said, "did you want Mavis?"

"You wouldn't understand."

"No, *she* wouldn't understand. She thinks you're one step below Jack the Ripper."

"I thought I was making headway. I'm working my way up to Guy Fawkes."

"I'm sorry, Junior. I figured, from the way she treats you like dirt — "

"Forget it!" I said.

Silence. Then I exploded. "God damn it, no, I won't forget it. I've been trying to get her to pay attention to me ever since the day she sent that cable for me."

"That's a different picture, kid," Clark said.

"And another thing," I went on. "Where did the two of you go during the air raid drill?"

"The bar."

"I guess if you're gonna do a blackout, that's the place to do it."

"Don't go making a joke out of it," Gable said angrily. "Do you want her or don't you? Because if you don't, I do."

"Just because she's homely?" I said.

"No," he said, "because she listens. Because — hell, I don't know any more. There's a war on." Silence. "Thanks for picking up dinner," he said.

"I didn't," said curtly. "The studio did. They have an account."

"You didn't sign my name to it, did you? They'll bill me."

"No," I said. "Greta Garbo."

Chapter 24

"WELL, WE CERTAINLY BOLLOXED things tonight," Mavis groaned as she unlocked the flat for herself and Elizabeth. Elizabeth had no immediate response as she kicked off her shoes, plopped onto the settee, and rubbed her sore feet.

"'We'?" Elizabeth mocked sharply. "You're the one who kidnapped him to the bar and tried to ingratiate yourself. You left me with the other one."

"All I was trying to do was make Captain Gable feel more comfortable with me so he'd then feel more comfortable with Colonel Hatcher. I wasn't trying to seduce him."

"That was hardly what it looked like to the other one and me," Elizabeth said. "You not only left the room, you did it during a drill. How much more obvious could you be?"

"It was Clark's idea," Mavis said.

"Oh, so now it's 'Clark' and not 'Captain Gable'," Elizabeth scored.

"You can't even remember the other one's name. His name is Alan Greenberg and he's a lieutenant."

"His name is Alan Greenberg and he's a bore. Do you know, he wouldn't let me get in a word all night? Every time I talked about my volunteer work at the hospital, he kept harping about Hollywood and some studio he works for."

"He works for Metro-Goldwyn-Mayer and he's been seconded to Clark for the duration."

"There you go with the Clark again."

"Do you want a drink?

Elizabeth weighed the answer. "I bloody well do."

Mavis Roberts and Elizabeth Manning had not known each other when the wartime housing office paired them as flat-mates in 1940. Most houses and apartments in England had been encouraged to take in borders, especially borders whose homes had been destroyed in the blitz. Unlike most of her friends, Manning had moved to London from the safety of Nottinghamshire to work for the Home Office. She had wanted to become involved in security but an almost immediate personality conflict with her superiors shifted her to a clerical position so, in order to feel more useful, she volunteered her spare time with the International Red Cross. The personality conflict didn't belong to her as much as it belonged to every man who dealt with her: they were drawn to her appearance and then repelled by her devotion to it. "She has such nice skin," one of them admired, "but look what it's stretched over."

Yet she was superbly organized and efficient, so management shifted her to a busier but lowlier clerical job, and there she stayed. Her meeting with Mavis came through a flat posting on the bulletin board. Because it was obvious to both Elizabeth and Mavis that Elizabeth was the more glamorous of the pair, there was no jealousy. If anything, when it came to social opportunities in a country invaded by men from all over the free world, Mavis enjoyed

Elizabeth's overflow. This is what irked Elizabeth so much regarding Gable. The tables weren't meant to be turned.

Mavis was unconcerned about such things. Her rise from informational officer to Colonel Hatcher's adjutant had been swift and remarkably unencumbered, despite her being a woman in a man's field. Born in Kent and raised by parents who valued education at a time when few options were accorded to them, and even fewer for girls, they instilled in young Mavis Carter Roberts a sense of self-worth that was pegged to what she knew, not what others thought. A move to London in 1939 coincided with the creation of the Ministry of Information shortly after Britain declared war on Germany. Taking the job of typist just to be able to put SPAM on the table, her penchant for correcting the grammatical mistakes of her superiors earned her an angry summons to her manager's office. Here her self-confidence saved her job when she explained clearly and unflinchingly to the man, a political appointee, that not only was it insulting to use the King's English poorly, it also opened him to misinterpretation, if not sacking. The man was insecure enough to swallow everything she told him, and he promoted her to his assistant. He didn't last, but she did, and was scooped up by the Ministry of Information in 1941. The roost with Hatcher's Chickens came about on a tour of the facilities when the Colonel heard the intelligent questions Mavis was asking and contrived to bring her under his unit.

Had Mavis lived in Hollywood and worn pants, she would have run a studio publicity department. Instead, she ran the 351st Bombardment Group's information office.

She didn't date servicemen. This was not a matter of protocol, ethics, or preference; it was a pragmatic personal decision. She had witnessed too many of them fail to return from missions and did not want to be a war widow. Instead, she was a war virgin.

Elizabeth, on the other hand, while not exactly opening up a new front, had neither illusions nor hesitation. She did not want a long-term relationship, and the uniformed eighteen-to-twenty-one-year-olds she encountered, often through Mavis, were likewise not interested in permanence. A kid going into battle wants to think about the future for his own peace of mind, but he also doesn't dare make long-range plans. Among the tragedies of war are the many ways it destroys people's sense of commitment.

So Mavis and Elizabeth shared, if not exactly friendship, then a state of symbiosis. The occasional bumps had managed to work themselves out in the past, but the Dorchester dinner kindled a new one. Elizabeth went in thinking she would be paired with Gable. So did Alan. If Mavis had intended to spirit Gable away for a private talk, she should have told both of them. Leaving Alan alone with Elizabeth seemed like a good idea. For one thing, Mavis figured, it might get Alan off her back as it was obvious that he was drawn to her. For another, her code of ethics would keep her from being attracted to either one of them, but particularly Gable.

Or was she, God forbid, falling for Gable anyway?

But the best-laid plans of mice and men, as Robbie Burns said, gang aft agley, and now Mavis had, as Elizabeth so clearly put it, bolloxed everything. The only way, she now imagined, to un-agley matters would be to treat Alan with a little more than respect and Gable with a little less than awe.

By the women's second Scotch they had settled their differences. By morning the whiskey buzz would be gone and the business buzz would begin.

Chapter 25

LEWKO HELD THE SLATE in front of the color camera, its striped clapstick raised and chalk lettering showing what he was about to read for the audio track.

"*Combat America*, forty-one B, take one."

Additional markings showed "DIR" for director, Clark Gable, and "CAM," for camera, Molina. Nobody had any fantasies about anyone's name appearing on the finished film — government films rarely contained credits — but it was a nice touch during production.

We were set up on the air field and had been there since three in the morning, waiting for the dawn. Contrary to legend, England does have a summer, and it promised to be beautiful for however short a time it was to last. England also has winter, and it seemed to return just before the summer sun rose. We needed the soft early rays not only to make Gable glow with gold but to subtly suggest optimism about the bombing sequence that was to come. We didn't actually know about a bombing sequence yet, but we knew that there would be one, so we were getting coverage now for later.

Combat America was scheduled to be shown in thousands of theatres in the States as soon it could be finished and prints could be delivered. The plan wasn't just for public information, it was to inspire young men to join the Army Air Corps and train for the 351st Bombardment group. That done, the picture would also give exhibitors and audiences a Clark Gable movie, even if he was just making guest appearances.

The documentary focused on the 351st Bombardment Group, but that was just an excuse to highlight Captain Gable. There was no advance script, only a strategy: We would tag along on missions like the one over Antwerp that nearly cost us our star until we had enough footage to piece together into sequences, then tie them together with Gable's narration to be recorded later.

The camera adjusted after Lewko's sync clap and turned to Gable, who was inside the nose turret housing of the B-17, his hands resting on its twin repeating guns. "This is the best seat in the house," he began, "if you're looking for action, real action — better'n any Hollywood movie I ever made."

The camera pulled back to reveal Gable squatting in the fullness of the turret, not fitting, the microphone boom barely out of sight above his head recording his words. Molina operated the blimped Mitchell while Battista recorded on his separate audio console. I knew we could never use the footage, but if it made Clark feel a part of things, good.

"This is the turret of a B-17 Flying Fortress," he explained. "In a couple of minutes we're gonna get in Hitler's face. You'll meet the ball turret gunner, Billy Murtaugh, age twenty. That's right: age twenty and he's seen it all. And if you like what you see, you can join in." Gable paused and looked over to me. I was standing beside the camera.

"Cut!" I said. I didn't expect to — it was Clark's job — but what the hell. "In fact, that's a print." Oh the power!

"Cheeky," said Clark as he climbed out of the turret and came out of the plane to join us. "Feel like a real director?"

"I'd like a little more emotion next time," I joked.

"Tell you what, Junior. You cram your ass in that fish bowl and see how much feeling you can generate. No wonder Billy's a little guy." He turned to the film crew. "Okay, break down the equipment and load it aboard. We can get some cutaways before take-off."

"I'll make sure they get cutaways of Murtaugh and the others. We need some faces," I said. Gable leaned down to me and said, in a low voice, "Don't waste film. I just mentioned his name to make the guys feel part of it. They'll probably cut out anything too personal." Then he announced in a louder voice, "And be sure to get reverse angles for coverage. Not just head-on shots."

"Is there anything you'd rather be doing besides directing?" I asked, trying to be cordial.

"Yeah," Clark growled. "Flying."

"Not gonna happen," I said. "Hatcher's orders."

"I wonder who leaned on him."

"I don't lean," I assured him. "Probably one of your supporters at the studio."

"Suit yourself," he said, "because if I don't get the footage, you'll have to."

"What do you mean?" I felt a twinge go through my chest.

"You don't think I'd send our guys up without supervision, do you?

"I'm not a director."

"You'll do till George Stevens comes along," Gable smiled. "Grab a camera and get me close-ups."

"You want me to go up there? In the air? Where they're shooting real bullets?"

"That's an order, lieutenant."

With that, Clark took a DR-70 camera from Molina, pressed it into my hands, and pushed me aboard. He followed me in and kept advancing against me through the fuselage until I was near the waist gunners. You don't want to rush haphazardly through a B-17; I dodged metal struts and sharp edges, looking back and ahead in a panic until he wasn't following me any more.

"You want point-of-view shots, Junior" he kept saying with each shove. "There's only one way to get 'em. You're about the right height: maybe it's time you did cram your ass where Murtaugh sits. Those'll be your cutaways." He backed me and the camera into the ball turret. Unlike him, I fit. I settled in, my hands touching the turret, and winced as I saw what was below me — rather, what wasn't below me. Talk about feeling exposed. Plexiglas all around, two huge guns just about growing out of my crotch, and the whole affair was vibrating even before the engines turned over. Or maybe it was just me shaking in fear.

"How does it feel, Junior," Clark asked.

"Stop calling me Junior."

"What's your problem?"

"I can hardly move in here."

Gable knocked me on the head. "Just roll film. These guys wanna take off."

I didn't see it, but Gable winked at Murtaugh and Murtaugh winked at Nelson. Nelson then nodded to Rudich and Rudich nodded to Andriotti. They checked to make sure Battista, Molina, Lewko and Jeffers were aboard, looked around to the rest of the crew, and signaled the ground staff to shut the door.

Nelson started the engines and I started to panic.

"What the hell's going on?" I screamed. "We're supposed to stay on the ground!" I tried to lift myself out of the turret but Gable put his foot on my chest to stop me.

"What about that dame?" he asked as we were taxiing toward the runway.

"What the hell are you doing?"

"Are you gonna ask her out again or what?"

I was frantic. "Is that all you can think about at a time like this? You shouldn't be on this flight."

"Put it in one of your cables back to the studio, you snitch," Gable said. "Don't you want excitement? What's got into you?"

"It's not what's into me, it's what I'm into. I'm in a ball turret, for Chrissake."

"Yup."

"Not funny, Clark. You promised to stay on the ground."

"I lied. Are you gonna call her for another date or what?"

I was confused. Fear does that. "Call who?"

"Mavis."

"I thought you wanted her."

"Do you want her?"

"You tricked me, you sonofabitch."

"That's the fighting spirit," he said, lifting me out of the turret compartment. "Now let's clock some air time."

We found seat belts and took off into the sunrise, me lecturing Clark about disobeying both Hatcher and Mayer. I still wasn't sure why Clark had become a cheerleader for Mavis, but I wasn't going to press him until we got back. Assuming we did.

Chapter 26

NELSON'S CREW HAD BEEN briefed about the mission's objective but Clark's crew had not on the sound theory that, since Gable wasn't going along, why get him involved? At five thousand feet and climbing, however, it occurred to Clark that this might be a good time to ask where we were all headed.

"All right, men, listen up," Captain Nelson said sharply into the intercom. "Our primary is the railroad station at Villacoublay. For those of you whose geography is rusty, that's in the northern part of France about two miles — check, three miles — from Versailles. It's a transfer point for Adolf's troops and ammo trains, and we can expect it to be heavily defended. So let's say a couple extra prayers."

Even though the interior of the Eightball was too noisy to record sound, Clark chatted up Billy Murtaugh. He had taken a liking to the kid whose sweet appearance covered expert aerial marksmanship talent and the unflinching nerve to wield it.

"I want to ask you a dumb question that ain't so dumb," Clark began. "Why are you here?"

Billy started to answer, then caught himself blushing when he realized whom he was talking to. "The way I see it, sir, I'm doing this for my country. I want to have a country to come back to. But maybe for my family in Lafayette. I want a family to come back to, too. Is that what you want to hear?"

"What I want is whatever you want to tell me, Billy. But I don't mean why are you in the Army, I mean why are you sitting behind that gunsight and not some other position?"

The boy paused. He knew a canned answer wouldn't work. "Because," he said, "because if I'm gonna get shot at, I wanna be able to shoot back, and if I'm gonna be wounded, I want it to finish me. No better place than this fish bowl."

"You grow up around guns?"

"Sure did. Back in Louisiana, goin' after cooter? Funny. I was goin' to go to school to be a veterinarian. Always liked animals. Me and my Pa, we never hunted for sport, just to put food on the table. Had a couple of dogs and lost 'em both, one to a water moccasin and the other to a truck. Don't guess I'll be a vet now."

Now it was Clark's turn to be silent. "Anything else, son?" he managed.

"Yeah. I'm gonna come back. Alive and whole. And if anybody out there wants to do this, tell 'em Uncle Sam's got plenty of planes, plenty of ammo, and plenty of Nazis." He grinned as wide as the size of his farm back home. "How'd I do?"

"Like a pro, kid. People get Oscars for less."

Gable worked his way through the crew. He asked Andriotti how he qualified as bombardier.

"They looked at my tests and figured I knew math," he said. "I never gave it much mind before, but they showed me a string of numbers and asked me what comes next, and I didn't even have to think about it, I just knew. So they gave me more tests, like how far ahead of a bird I'd have to shoot, and how to feel the wind. Maybe they think I'm part Indian. I'm not, I'm all Italian. But me and this newfangled bombsight, sir, I seem to be able to do what they want."

"And what do they want, Larry?" Gable pressed.

"They want me to drop bombs on soldiers and not civilians, sir," he said by rote.

"And how's that going?"

He took a while answering. "That's sorta between me and God."

I was fascinated with the instant intimacy that Clark was able to achieve with average people. That was his appeal on the screen, but he had it in real life without a script. He could ask anybody any question and they'd want to answer. He seldom spoke about himself except to be self-deprecating — very rare for a celebrity — and was genuinely interested in other people. He hid the pain he was carrying over Carole and turned it around into a raging curiosity about the world that she would never get to see. I saw it bubble up every time he set his jaw before entering a meeting. And when he looked out of the aircraft's open gunnery doors. Look down and you see the ground not far below, maybe a mile. Look straight out and you see the other planes in the sortie. Because we weren't alone up there. There must have been twenty other aircraft, all Flying Fortresses, heading to France. Then it hit me that this was not an attempt at intimidating the enemy by sending a vast number of bombers into occupied territory. It was a calculated exercise in percentages by High Command counting on some of us getting through and others of us not coming back.

"Messerschmitts at nine o'clock," the starboard waist gunner shouted. Nelson was quick to respond. "Battle stations!" he ordered. The waist gunners, tail gunners, and all of us locked and loaded. And waited.

I turned to Molina. "Hand me something to shoot with!" I was thinking of a rifle. He tossed me a Bell & Howell.

Murtaugh waited for the Messerschmitt to get in range. It didn't. Instead, it rolled over and around the Eightball like a spider preparing to spin a cocoon. Nelson made eye contact with the pilot, who smiled and tipped his wing. He then circled the B-17 and left. "Sonofabitch," said Nelson. "What gives."

"Why doesn't he fire?" said a shocked Lewko.

"He wants to see what we've got," answered Rudich.

"Why don't *we* fire?" said Lewko.

"We're in formation," Andriotti said, nodding in every direction. "We'd hit our own."

"So what do we do?"

"Our job."

More Messerschmitts arrived, flying out of a cloud, led by the one that had just saluted us. They flew so close to our formation that none of us could shoot at them. Nelson took to the radio. "All right, let's stop the funny stuff. Break formation."

Each B-17 knew what to do. Some descended, some climbed, and others turned.

I asked nobody in particular "Where's our cover?"

"It's just us, Junior," answered Gable, for the first time looking concerned.

Nelson pushed the throttle and took us up. It was a steep climb, and Jeffers was knocked to the floor, He crawled across to the port side waist gunner and lifted the camera to get footage when the gunner let loose a volley shouting "Here they come. Port side, port side!"

"Taking evasive action," Nelson shouted. There was little a B-17 could do but power ahead. The German fighters picked the lead B-17 as target. They dove and twisted around it, firing promiscuously. Rounds tore into its wing but it kept going. Amazing machines.

Another one fired at us. Rounds whizzed past the starboard openings and I heard a metallic noise. My cheek hurt. A shell had glanced off the camera I was holding to my eye and I'd felt the spark burn in. Clark was on it. "You're fine," he said. "But your camera's getting a Purple Heart."

Battista spoke for the first time. "Why can't we drop the payload?"

Gable answered, "Look at the cloud cover. We might be over civilian targets. We can't drop our bombs unless we're sure."

Molina screamed. "Here they come again."

"Hang on!" Gable shouted.

Nelson banked the plane hard to starboard and rolled into a dive. This put us at an even lower altitude where our gunners had clear shots all around. They didn't hesitate to fire, but it was like swatting flies with a soda straw.

Gable shouted down to Murtaugh.

"Billy, how's it going?"

He was making too much noise to hear.

In the cockpit, Rudich told Nelson, "We're forty miles from the primary."

"Roger."

One of the German planes fired at the cockpit. Nelson saw it and veered, but one round hit the nose ball. It hit a metal strut and pinged off. "You okay?" Nelson asked Rudich. A solid knock on the fuselage served as Yes.

"Pilot to bombardier," Nelson said. "Prepare to drop bombs if the clouds break."

"Aye-aye, sir," shouted Andriotti, and reached for the lever that opened the bomb bay. "Oh shit."

"Good Christ," I said, "you didn't just remember to draw a picture of Hitler on them, are you?"

Before Andriotti could answer, a string of bullets ripped through in and out of the Plexiglas and smacked into Andriotti's shoulder, ripping a hole in his jump suit. It happened too fast for me to recoil. It happens faster than you think.

"Larry!" I called out.

He looked surprised. This wasn't supposed to happen. His face went white. "Damn it," he said.

Nelson heard him. "Report!"

"Shoulder. Not sure how bad. It's starting to hurt." I tried to hold him, but he grabbed my shirt and pulled me down to him. "You gotta help me."

I said I'd get the medical kit. He said, "No! Open the bomb bay. The rounds severed the cable. You have to do it there."

"Where" I asked.

"The bomb bay. There's a lever — move it across."

I tried to lift him out but he was in too snugly.

"You can't miss it," Andriotti said. "Pull it and — " he coughed and then yelled at the pain his spasm caused. I said I'd get somebody to help.

"You do it," the kid said. "Do something for a change except take pictures."

"How do I know it didn't work?" I asked. "Maybe it opened."

"You'd feel the drag on the plane," Andriotti said. "Move your ass."

Nelson chimed in. "He's down. You're not. What's the problem?"

I don't know what possessed me, but I said, "No problem, sir!"

Nelson was astonished. "Greenbaum?"

"Greenberg," I said. "He doesn't think the bomb bay doors are open."

"They're not," Nelson said. "Cable's gone. You'll have to do it manually."

"Yes, sir," I heard myself say. I don't know why, but I did. Andriotti was taking shallow breaths as I climbed over him and crawled below deck to the bomb compartment. I lowered myself into the open space where the bombs lived.

If you've never balanced yourself on a piece of metal with nothing beneath you except your genitals followed by a couple of tons of explosives, a metal hatch cover, and below it the ground, while you are being shot at, I don't recommend going out of your way to seek the experience. For one thing, it's cold as a bastard, and I couldn't feel the ends of my fingers as I looked for a way to manually open the flaps.

Nelson's voice: "We're approaching the drop zone. What the hell's going on? Greenbaum, for Chrissake, report!"

"Greenberg!" I shouted back, even though nobody could hear me through the engine noise and the deafening wind.

"If the clouds break, we let 'em go."

There was a metal lever just beneath the hatch cover. It was the only thing that looked like it could be pulled. I figured it would either open the bomb day doors or let go the bombs themselves or both, and me with them. There was no place to stand. I hung onto a metal strut with one hand and yanked the lever with the other. It slipped out of my grip. I tried to angle myself where I could get better purchase.

Suddenly I wasn't alone. Clark had lowered himself into the bomb compartment and was also reaching for the release lever. At six-foot-one he was a head taller than me, and it was an important head. He stretched, found the lever, and pulled it hard. The bomb bay flaps opened and the rush of air nearly sucked me out of the plane. Clark grabbed me and hoisted me to safety, back into the body of the aircraft. I lay panting on the floor and cautiously rolled over to gander down. The wind sanded against my face and, as thin as the air was, it smelled clean and innocent.

Beneath us were thick clouds, and beneath them was Villacoublay. Clark and I raced back to Andriotti. He had pulled himself to the bombsight and was trying to press the release button.

"As you were!" Nelson's voice shouted throughout the plane. "Hold your fire!" Andriotti passed out and fell to the floor. The bombs did not drop. The clouds did not yield. Mission aborted. The disappointment singed the air like a burned match.

"Let's make like a baby and head out," Nelson said wearily over the plane's intercom. "The people whose lives we saved just now will never know how close they came. This is what separates us from the enemy."

We turned around and headed home. Meanwhile, we were still being tailed by half a dozen enemy aircraft. Murtaugh sprayed the sky with rounds, wildly swaying his gun side to side. Somehow it worked. Screaming like a man on a mission, he picked off, first, one, and then a second attacking plane with a single sustained burst until he had to reload. The crew cheered him just as another enemy plane flew out of a cloud, straight for him, and fired.

The ball turret blew open and Murtaugh's flesh exploded with it leaving a fine mist of blood trailing the Eightball as the German plane banked and rolled back into its cloud.

Chapter 27

THE ATTACK CONTINUED. YOU had to hand it to the three re-maining German flyers for not giving up despite drawing concen-trated return fire from the rest of the Flying Fortresses. The one that got Billy Murtaugh re-emerged from its cloud and paced us slightly to the rear, just out of angle from both waist gunners.

Evasive action for a B-17 is like asking an elephant to share a phone booth. All we could do was keep chugging back to England and hope that the Messerschmitts either ran out of fuel, spent their ammunition, or got bored. But then I realized why this particular one was dogging us: Clark had been holding onto the port side opening and was looking the German pilot squarely in the eye. The German pilot saw glory. Gable saw revenge.

The Messerschmitt throttled back and peeled away to gain alti-tude and distance, then turned to come directly at us. Was he crazy? Was it worth his life to make a kill? Even before he flew into target range, Clark set sights on him and started firing. The German fired back, then ran out of ammo. Clark didn't. He kept firing and drove a perfect row of rounds across the Messerschmitt's window, tearing the pilot's head off and exploding the aircraft into a huge fireball that would have engulfed us if we hadn't been moving. We watched the debris fall from the sky.

Gable turned to the waist gunner. "Thanks for lending me your weapon."

"No sweat," said the stunned young man.

A squawk came over the speaker system. "Escort leader to Operation Thirty. Escort leader to Operation Thirty. We have confirmed enemy planes either shot down or in full retreat. Return to base. Repeat, return to base. Over."

We landed with our payload intact and our crew in mourning. We had saved lives who would never know we spared them, and lost two that we would miss forever. Only then did Clark and I see the full damage. One of the other men had covered Andriotti's body. The boy had lost too much blood to make it. I looked into the ball turret where Murtaugh had been. There wasn't enough left to bury. Jeffers pointed his camera at Gable to capture his reaction. Gable blocked the lens with his hand. "Hasn't there been enough shooting today?" he said emotionlessly.

HOWARD STRICKLING
MGM STUDIOS, CULVER CITY, CALIFORNIA
VIA TELEX. CENSOR APPROVED.
CLARK IS REAL-LIFE HERO BUT HE WON'T
ADMIT IT,
SAYING EVERYBODY IS A HERO IN THIS WAR.
GREENBERG.

What I didn't — couldn't — tell Strickling was that the Army confiscated our footage without even processing it. They also wouldn't let me tell Metro they did. I can't blame them. John Huston reported the same situation when he was filming 'The Battle of San Pietro" in Italy and the Army censor removed shots of soldiers being shot on camera. In his case they didn't burn the footage, they just filed it away for later which, in a government bureaucracy, amounts to pretty much the same thing.

I sent the Telex from Hatcher's office. Mavis was good enough to type it for me. She also was the one who censored it.

"Can I at least add some color to the report?" I asked her.

"Be my guest," she said.

I started dictating. "Clark is writing the parents of the fallen men. Ordinarily the Commanding Officer would do that, but Gable watched them die and feels he should be the one to shoulder the responsibility. It's no use grounding him. He thinks it's a game. Taking risks is what you do in a war, he insists. He's even got me taking risks. That's right, I'm taking life or death risks."

I threw that last sentence in for Mavis's sake, not MGM's.

"I heard you the first time," she said, "and I didn't put it in then, either."

I ignored her and, as long as she was ignoring me, I tried something else. "I also think I'm becoming attracted to Colonel Hatcher's civilian adjutant. Don't worry, she's a girl. In fact, she's a lady, except she barely notices me when she's around Clark."

Mavis stopped typing before she got to the end of the sentence. "All right, I think we can dispense with that. Perhaps I even owe you an apology."

I was stunned.

"I thought that you and Elizabeth might have some interests in common. That's why I asked her to come along on our fateful dinner date. I think it's fair to say that you didn't find her company amusing."

"Amusing isn't the word I would have chosen. I'm sure she's a lovely woman once you get to know her."

"She is. If you'd taken the time to listen to her instead of monopolizing the conversation, you might have."

"Monopolizing? From the moment we sat down she didn't stop talking. After a while I just stared at her, wondering how she was getting air."

For the first time I saw Mavis baffled. "You mean she did all the talking?"

"Like she was vaccinated with a Victrola needle."

"She told me that you were the one who wouldn't let her speak."

"Hardly," I said. "In fact, I think I deserve a Purple Heart for holding in my sarcasm. How do I fold thee gauze? Let me count the ways."

"Oh, dear," Mavis said. "This does put a new light on things."

"At least you had a good time with Clark."

"That wasn't my plan."

"I don't understand. Did you plan on a *bad* time with Clark?"

"No, no, no," she corrected. "I just wanted time-time with Clark. He started telling me about the pressure of trying to do something for his country but not being permitted to because he was famous. I realized that he was trying to reconcile his helplessness over Miss Lombard with his power as a star. What he needs is a woman."

"And what are you?" I asked.

"A military adjutant first and a woman second, and he seems to need me."

I was getting angry. "Let him find his own! Of all the men in the known universe, he will have the least trouble finding a woman. He's Clark Gable!"

"Aren't you forgetting something? It's the woman's decision. Look at the way you're trying to corral me."

"And what good does it do? What chance do I have against Clark Gable? Is there a woman alive who can resist him? Even when he just stands there with his mouth shut he sends out mating calls. I've seen it."

Mavis pushed herself away from the Telex and pinned me against the wall sitting in her swivel chair. "I forbid you self-pity, let alone jealousy!" she started. "Clark is desperately lonely. You're either too young or too American to see that. Sometimes a man just needs to talk, and there are things a man can tell a woman that he can't tell another man, even drunk."

I'd had it. "Does he tell you before or after you make love?"

Mavis stood up, slapped me hard across my face, and turned her back.

"I deserved that," I said, feeling genuine regret.

"I agree," she said curtly. Then she softened. "But if it makes you feel any better — and I hope it doesn't — he and I just talk. About Carole."

I took a step toward her. "Mavis — "

She stopped me. "No. No second chance. At least, not right now. I think you need to go."

And I did.

Chapter 28

Combat America had more hands going over it than the sweetheart of Sigma Chi. Commissioned by General Arnold, the picture was described as a recruiting film for gunners. Other than promising kids a chance to kill krauts, what else could a movie possibly offer? We shot footage of local tourist attractions, spent time with civilians (especially the pretty ones), gave insider looks at training exercises and combat missions, and, in general, tried to convey the excitement and, yes, even the danger. Recruitment works because no eighteen-year-old sees himself dying, and thus the adventure of the war is what draws them in. The reality comes later, and it can land pretty heavily.

Informational films are a special animal. When our MGM short subjects department makes them, we know that we can never convey specific information, so what we try to do is impart a sense of whatever the film is about. If it's a profile of various occupations, we show how intriguing they are. If it's a travelogue, we show people enjoying visiting them. If it's home improvements, we show how easy it is, then suggest they learn how to do it on their own time, and so forth.

In the armed forces, it's the Army Signal Corps that is tasked with single-subject training films: how to fold a parachute, how to purify water, how to use a compass, and, of course, how to keep from getting the clap. Those are rarely shown to the general public. *Combat America* is not one of those restricted titles, although we did shoot a Scottish instructor briefing the men about the monetary exchange rate (one British pound equaled four U.S. dollars) before they were to head out to the local pub. He also briefed them on something more important: enemy agents among us. "The dumb spies have all been shot," he said coldly. "The smart ones are still living."

One of the most important tasks we had was working guest appearances by top brass into the finished film. "How are you coming with this camera training film of yours?" General Eaker asked Gable in a pre-arranged "casual" encounter we shot on the base. Ira C. Eaker is Commanding General of the 8th Air Force, of which the 351 is a part.

"A little too early to tell yet, sir," Captain Gable responded crisply. "We're turning a camera on everything and everybody."

Eaker was well-rehearsed. "I know what General Arnold had in mind," he recited to his famous screen partner. "Having to make those gunners practice. Captain Gable, our gunners are already the best in the business, but if they were ten percent better, it would cost the enemy another hundred fighters a month."

"So fire away, gunners," Gable responded in recorded narration paying off the scene. "Plenty more practice before that first mission."

The combat footage that we had already shot — that which was not confiscated by military intelligence — was logged and stored for later editing. Meanwhile, our Little Hollywood Group rolled film on anything that gave a sense of what American flyers would encounter when they arrived in England. The RAF had formally turned over the airfield to us but continued to fly at night. The U.S. sorties were carried out by day. We also practiced identifying airborne equipment — no longer by memorizing silhouettes in books but by watching fly-bys of an actual captured twin engine Junkers JU 388 and a deadly and versatile Heinkel 111.

The toughest part about combat is waiting. Waiting for a mission, and then waiting to start the mission, and then waiting to get to the target, and then, worst of all, waiting to get back safely. Clark wanted to show the ritual of waiting, and he did it by talking to the men who were doing it. There was the truck driver from New York; a kid trying to concentrate on a poker hand; an ambulance driver trying to keep casual; the ground crews who count the returning planes to see if any are missing. "You can uncross your fingers now," Gable says.

We shot footage of planes returning from those missions. Some had engines out and yet could still fly; credit both the designer and the pilot. One couldn't get its bomb day doors closed. Another caught a bullet in his radio. Clark named as many of the men as he could for the pride of their families back home.

"How was it?" Gable asked two men who were cleaning their rifles on returning from the sky.

"You know what, Captain?" said one of them by the name of Kenny. "I don't think those Germans like us."

"Are you ready to go again?" Clark asked.

"Sure," he said. "We want to get this thing over."

"Did you learn anything you didn't know before?"

"Plenty," said the other kid, named Phil. "At home they told us the Gerries made most of their attacks on the tail. Today most of 'em were on the nose."

"Yeah," Kenny added. "Most of the time I had my turrets pointed at twelve o'clock. I musta fired a thousand rounds."

One of the more unusual interviews came when Clark spoke to a man dressed in white and standing unhappily over a stove. "Hello, Sergeant Moseby," he asked. "What's this?" and pointed to the pots and pans. "I thought you were a ball turret gunner."

"I thought so too, sir, but I've been grounded," the man said.

"Your past crept up on you, huh?" Gable asked knowingly.

"Yes sir," the man said. "They found out I was chef at the Brown Derby in Hollywood and they have me in the mess making a cake tonight for the officers' party." He and Gable already knew each other from California.

"Anything you can do about getting back into combat?"

"I don't think so, Captain," Moseby said wearily.

"Well, Sergeant," Gable said cheerfully, "remember this. There are two kinds of cakes., One of them's good, and the other one — I'll be seeing you."

But there was precious little humor in the film; combat is no laughing matter. We filmed arrivals of flights where their crew members had been killed. Removing bodies from aircraft and helping others into ambulances. Groups of buddies unable to comfort each other, just staring in shock and loss.

Clark made it a point to visit military hospitals. On one such occasion, he ran into Lieutenant Bob Wallace who was looking forward to getting back into action.

"How are you doing?" Clark asked the young man, who was sitting with a nurse on a bench overlooking a stream. Wallace introduced the nurse as Miss O'Neil. "How do you do?" Clark said.

"Wally, I never got a chance to ask you," Clark said. "Tell me just what happened when you got hit."

"Well," the flyer said, "we left the target and we were on our way home. We got to the coast and we had our guns stowed away when a couple of FWs snuck up on us and gave us a good burst."

"Oh, I see, you had your guns stowed away, eh?" Clark said. "That was a little early, wasn't it?"

"It certainly was," Wallace admitted.

"It's not a good idea to relax over here till you get back to your own base," Gable said, making a point often stressed in training: Like a reporter who's still on the record even after he closes his notebook, a soldier at war is never off duty. The two men shared their thoughts about the importance of first aid training, and then Clark asked, "What do you and your men think of the B-17s?"

"They're the best equipment in the world," the young man endorsed.

We alternated between combat footage, scenes of life on base, tourist footage from the surrounding village, and even a dose of religion as we shot soldier Pete Provenzale singing "Ave Maria" at a church service the day before going back up into the air on a mission.

One of the most moving moments was an award ceremony held on the air field. We wanted to honor the men we had seen earlier, such as pilot Peters, gunner Provenzale, turret gunners Philip and Kenneth Hulls, bombardier Stevens, and tail gunner Tuchet, among others in the 351st. Clark wanted to sound upbeat and struck the balance in typical Gable style: "You can't get out of it, you know. They pin medals on you for this sort of work. It's not so much a thrill for you," he said self-effacingly, "but what a great kick it will hand the folks back home. The silver star. The distinguished flying cross. The soldier's medal. Dad, Ma, and that certain girl." Even Hatcher got a medal for commanding a mission.

Combat America was shaping up to be a solid public relations film. So far, we had recklessly grabbed aerial footage wherever and whenever we could; the polished shooting was all done on the ground. Then one morning we were told to being our equipment and our rear ends to the briefing room. We weren't told why, but we could guess. We were about to shoot a mission from beginning to end — not our end, we hoped and prayed.

Chapter 29

TWO IN THE MORNING. None of us could sleep. Something was up on the air field. You could hear the ground crew revving the great engines of the fleet all night long, but no planes were taking off. In the morning, we went out to try to see what had been going on. We found vast new stockpiles of bombs set up on the grass on either side of the runways and saw extra bomb racks installed on the planes. It didn't take a genius to figure out that the 351st was getting ready for a major operation.

More brass began arriving. You could count the flags and stars on the vehicles lined up in the parking area. There was no formal greeting ceremony; officers arrived, proceeded immediately to the Old Man's (Hatcher's) office, and three hours later you'd see food sent in. How long would it be before they told us what was going on?

Word passed among the men faster than the latest traveling salesman joke. Taking the confab as an omen, many of the guys figured it was a good time to write letters home. They couldn't say what was happening or even that they suspected something was about to happen; their letters would never make it through V-mail. It was like being a runner at a track and field event. Your feet are on the starting blocks, the official is poised with his pistol in the air, and he's saying, "On your mark. Get set. Are you set? Are you on your mark? Okay, on your mark — " while your entire being tensed and waited for him to say "go."

On the morning of August 17, they shook us awake at 3 AM with orders to assemble an hour later. At the briefing, the General said we were leaving on a big mission and asked for guesses what the target was. Even those of the men who had shaken the sleep from their heads by then only came close. Instead, he uncovered a map of Europe with the 351st flight path already drawn in ink. It was to be a daring bifurcated sortie under the name of Mission 84. It had been postponed several times because of foul weather, but this was the day it would finally take place. The "double-strike mission" would involve 376 bombers, half of which would head for Schweinfurt, Germany, and then return to England while the other half would hit Regensburg, Germany, and continue to Northern Africa to surprise Rommel. The strategy was to create such a massive assault that the Luftwaffe would be unable to commit enough planes to fight on two aerial fronts.

"Stations at 5:05," the commander said, "start-up at 6:05, taxi at 6:15 and take-off at 6:30." The men scrambled to their posts with a mixture of excitement and anxiety, but mostly relief that they were finally going to make a major assault on the Nazi war machine.

As Clark and I left the briefing room, Hatcher stopped us. "Where are you two going?"

"Apparently to Germany," Gable said.

"No you're not," the Colonel said firmly. "You're grounded. Greenbaum too."

Clark said nothing, but he also didn't move. Nor did Hatcher who, reading the silence, continued.

"Orders from General Arnold," he said. "This is going to be a rough one. We expect a calculated loss of men and planes, and the Army Air Corps doesn't want you to be among them."

"Permission to speak freely, sir?" Gable asked.

"No!" Hatcher shot back. "You're just gonna hand me some line about coming here to fight and how you want to be treated just like everyone else. Well get this: you're not like everyone else, Captain. You are Clark fucking Gable. Maybe all the guys out there figure they don't have a chance of ever being like you, but if you don't comeback they'll sure as hell get the idea they can be killed like you." Then he looked at me. "And your little dog, too."

Clark must have heard tirades like this from Mr. Mayer, but with someone like Hatcher he couldn't call his agent to complain. He had to take it, and take it he did. "Yes, sir," he said passionlessly.

"I'm sorry, Clark," Hatcher warmed. "I've also been instructed to tell you that you'll be confined to quarters until the planes return. General Arnold doesn't want another gambit like the one you and your orderly pulled over Villacoublay." Hatcher looked at me the way a dog regards a flea. It crossed my mind that Green*baum* the orderly might be grounded but that Green*berg* the lieutenant was not. Then I thought, "What the hell am I thinking?"

"Dismissed," Hatcher said. Clark and I both saluted and left the building .

Clark and I walked without saying anything. Finally I asked, "How do you feel?"

"Useless," he said without having to think about it. "I always thought that being famous allowed you to get things done. Charities, favors, helping people. It's not about getting good seats at restaurants. But I never thought it would get in the way of fighting for my country. "

"Not every fight involves bullets," I said. "Imagine the good that your film'll do when it hits a thousand screens."

Gable withdrew into silence until we reached our quarters. "You've got a point, Junior," he said impatiently. "Let's hope they bring back enough footage so we can make them the film they don't even know they want."

It was a tough wait. After take-off, the 351st rendezvoused with other flights for the foray into German air space. At an altitude of ten thousand feet, the condensation on their wings formed white trails that spotters on the ground could see. Three hours out, the T-47 Thunderbolt escorts turned back and the formation was on its own. Before long, the enemy appeared. Their wings were also leaving trails, and the 351st's gunners spotted them.

The hand-held, silent color footage shot by our camera crew and those aboard other bombers told the story, and we would stitch it together later. The Norden bomb sights performed perfectly and hundreds of explosive and incendiary bombs pummeled the airdrome fields, hangars, and repair shops of Regensburg.

The German fighter planes did their job no less well than our bombers. They paralleled the formation, then slowed to shoot from behind. A few performed suicide dives to try to knock ours out of the sky. The Flying Fortresses' tight formation made them almost invulnerable, although three were lost in the raid and a number of others sustained damage.

"It's thunder out of the Allegheny, Adolf," Clark would read on the narration that would be matched to the stunning aerial footage (some of which would be augmented by pick up shots on the ground). "You said Americans were soft and decadent? Well here's a red, white, and blue headache that'll help you change your mind."

What he didn't say, and what we could not show in the film, was that the contingent of bombers sent to Schweinfurt suffered extensive losses, so much so that the bomber group had to postpone a scheduled second attack on the target some weeks later that might have inflicted terminal damage on Germany's industrial war machine.

Clark was upset by the grounding decree and didn't want to discuss it with Mavis, me, or anyone. It also distanced him from Lewko, Molina, Jeffers, and Battista, to whom he had grown close in the last year and a half. It burned and embarrassed him that they were still taking the risks that he was being denied. The less he tried to feel special, the more the Army treated him as someone who was.

Chapter 30

ONE NIGHT CLARK OUTFITTED himself in impeccable civvies, walked to the gate on the base, and hailed a passing Army truck. "You heading into town?" he asked.

"Sure," the driver said, blinking twice. He'd heard that Clark Gable was stationed somewhere in those walls but never that he would use his lorry to escape them. All he could say was, "Hop aboard." His elation turned to confusion when Clark walked behind the vehicle and hopped in the back with a bunch of other guys hitching a ride.

I didn't intend to go into town. I had homework. I even had to skip the movies at the base theatre. It was a double feature of *The More the Merrier* and *Shadow of a Doubt*, but I didn't feel like watching two great filmmakers (George Stevens and Alfred Hitchcock) when I was trying to save *Combat America* from the scrap heap.

By this time we had assembled all the footage from our bombing raid, the interviews with enlisted men and officers, beauty shots from the local community, and posed scenes of Clark and other notables. We had a rough cut and I decided to grit my teeth and see how it looked with some of the cut-together footage. My goal was not so much to see if the 351st came off well but to make sure Clark Gable did.

I ran the assembly cut on a double-system unit that looked like two projectors pasted together. One half was a 16mm projector that handled the picture, and the other half played back the sound in sync. It burned me that it was manufactured by a German company named Siemens, but you can't have everything. Ordinarily I would have watched it on a Movieola but I needed to see it on a big screen to check for flaws that couldn't be seen clearly enough on a Movieola image the size of a playing card.

Viewing uncut footage can be depressing; you see all the camera shakes, the false starts, the bloopers, and, worst of all, the waste of expensive film stock while the camera runs waiting for something to happen.

As foot after foot rolled through the projector onto the screen, I realized that most of it focused on Clark. It was as though they were filming World War II starring Clark Gable. I made a mental note to ask them to downplay Clark and stress the regular men. It was also hard looking at faces that I knew had been shot down.

Then I did something I had never done before, even in the rare private screenings I'd had at MGM: I stood up and walked toward the screen, letting the projected image shine on me. When you're alone in a screening room with a larger-than-life image being projected on the screen, it becomes more than a feeling of intimacy, it becomes an enveloping sense of the present. When my shadow was the same size as Gable's, I stared at him. He glowed off the screen. In my mind, I put myself in the scene with him. If he faced screen left, I faced screen right and we stood opposite each other. If he faced the camera, I faced the screen. All along, I told myself, "Okay, I'm not Clark Gable, I'm not Clark Gable. But that doesn't mean I have to give up Mavis without a fight." Clark couldn't get off the screen, but I could leave the room. I knew what I had to do. I took a bus into town.

"You can't be here." Mavis looked down and saw the box of chocolates, bag of sugar, and bottle of Scotch I was carrying, and she still said, "You can't be here."

I said, "Well, I am."

I walked past her and into her flat, already off-loading the provisions.

"I don't want your gifts," she said, taking the sugar off her kitchen counter and putting near the door. "Take all this and go. I am not some urchin you can buy with tins of food or a starlet you can compromise with the promise of a screen test."

"I never said you were," I stated, moving the sugar back on the counter. "But I do know what you are. Do you want to hear what you are?"

"No. Get out."

"Not until I tell you what you are. Do you know what you are? You are a royal pain in the ass."

"I can't stand you either."

I held her and kissed her. On the lips. She didn't struggle.

"Feeling better?" she asked. I nodded. Then she swung at me. This time I was ready for her and ducked.

"Stop being so British. Didn't you feel anything?"

She practically fumed. "What do you think this is, one of your Hollywood movies? Where the man pursues the woman and she eventually gives in because she secretly loves him? I should have you arrested for assault. Life isn't like a movie, Alan."

"To hell with life," I said. "You're the one who's living in a god damned movie! You're going out with Clark Gable."

"We are not going out. I told you, we just spend time together. He needs to be with me."

"You're no shrink," I sputtered.

"And you're no Clark Gable!" She aimed it squarely at me and hit home. Then she winced and said, "That was a cheap shot, wasn't it?"

"No," I said, genuinely hurt. "It was an expensive shot. Right in my heart."

Her tone softened but she kept her distance. "Alan, I don't fool myself into thinking I'm Greer Garson or Loretta Young. I'm certainly no Carole Lombard. He knows that. This is not for me. It's for him."

"Do you expect me to believe you're not getting anything out of it?"

"A brief encounter," she said. I think I even saw a tear starting. "Nothing more. Certainly no one will believe me once he's left. We both know that. The war has changed so much over here, especially for women. I wonder how the war has changed you."

"Do you really want to know?" I was challenging her.

"If you'd like to tell me."

I motioned for us to sit down. I took the easy chair and she sat safely across the room on a couch. "In Hollywood everybody wants something. My job is to give it to them. Autographed pictures? No problem. Advance book galleys? Home phone numbers? Party girls? Call Greenberg. If the studio was sick and needed an enema, Alan Greenberg is where they'd stick the nozzle. And how do they show their gratitude? They gave me a choice of keeping Clark Gable out of battle or going to jail for doing exactly what they hired me to do. Sure, I've done those things. For them! I don't even know enough to be ashamed of it. But one thing I'm not ashamed of is knowing you. You are the one person I've met here that I have never tried to —."

It wasn't working. I was being honest and it wasn't working.

Mavis was staring at me like I was trying to con her. Maybe I was and didn't know it. Maybe I'd been conning people so long that I honestly didn't realize when I was doing it.

"Or maybe I'm so far gone that—" I picked up, practically pleading with her to believe me, "Mavis, I just know that I —"

I didn't get to finish. There was a knock at the door. I didn't have to answer it to know who it was, but I did anyway. It was Clark. My taxi had made it into town before his truck ride. Gable looked at me, then at Mavis, then saw her tear, and he quickly comprehended. I knew I was finished, so I brushed past him and left down the stairs.

"Wait a minute, Junior," he said.

"Forget it," I threw back as I hit the bottom stair.

"Dammit, Lieutenant, that's an order!"

I stopped in my tracks. He looked at me from the landing. I refused to look at him. It was very dramatic.

"Do you want her or not?

"It's her choice."

"That's not a Yes," he said.

I couldn't face him. "Why? What chance do I have?"

"None, if you don't take it." He didn't move. "Well?"

I didn't answer. I opened the front door and left. I hope I didn't slam it behind me.

Only when I'd left did Gable step into Mavis's flat. By now she was in tears. Clark held her gently. "I've been telling you everything that's been on my mind," he said. "Is there something you want to tell me that's on yours?"

Mavis shook her head No. Clark put his hand under her chin and gently lifted her head to peer into her eyes. Even the most jaded observer would have sworn it was as romantic as anything they'd ever seen on a movie screen.

Actors in a love scene see things differently. Part of it is technical: They have to stare into the correct eye so it looks right on screen, they must not press their lips together too firmly lest it appear vulgar, and, above all, they have to think about the person they really love while acting with the person they're appearing with. Gable did it better than anybody; that's why he was the king. And he also knew when his co-star was faking. Mavis wasn't faking, but it was clear that her mind was elsewhere.

"Do you want me to go after him?" Clark asked.

"No."

"Do you want both of us to go after him?"

"No."

"Do you even know what you want?"

"No. Yes. I just want to be somewhere else. Somewhere there's people."

"All right, then," Gable said. "We're out for a good, clean time. If you change your mind and want Alan, let me know and we'll find him. Meanwhile, I'm on a six-hour pass. After that I'm AWOL and they lock me in the brig, and you'll have to find Alan on your own."

Maybe it was a new experience for Clark to be with a woman whose mind was somewhere else. But his mind had been so many elsewhere places, he figured he could deal with it when they went out. He helped Mavis with her hat and coat.

Chapter 31

THEIR FIRST STOP WAS a return visit to the Dorchester. They headed toward the cocktail lounge but as they crossed the lobby a familiar voice — familiar to Clark — called out to him.

"Clark? Jumping Jehoshaphat, what are you doing here?"

Gable stiffened. He weighed ignoring it, but it had a level of authority that made him pause long enough to connect memories. Mavis saw this and whispered, "Do you want to keep walking or shall I wait for you across the lobby?"

"We've already been seen together," he said, "but if it's who I think it is, he's going to talk my ear off until I can break away. Wait for me in the bar."

"I can't," Mavis said. "Unescorted women aren't allowed into the lounge. They think we're slags. You call them — "

"I know what we call them," Clark said. "All right, have a seat and watch the show."

Mavis smiled and walked off just as an ebullient, dark-skinned man with thinning black hair and extraordinarily bright eyes approached him, all handshakes. This was Frank Capra, who had directed Gable to an Oscar in *It Happened One Night* and was now in charge of the United States Government's wartime propaganda filmmaking.

"Frank, you old conniver!" Gable smiled. "Aren't you supposed to be at Fort Roach making 'Why We Fight'"?

"Yes, but I came over to see how Jack Ford, George Stevens, and Willy Wyler are doing. You know Willy here."

Capra led Gable to the library where William Wyler, whose drawn features and intensity were offset by a conspiratorial smile, was already rising to greet him. "How do you do, Clark."

"I sure admire your work, Mr. Wyler," Gable said. "I heard you were making one of Frank's documentaries."

Wyler's smile dropped. "It's my documentary," he corrected. "You sound like Sam Goldwyn. Somebody once mentioned William Wyler's *Wuthering Heights* in front of him and Sam exploded. 'I made *Wuthering Heights*,'" he said. "'Wyler only directed it.' I'm doing a film on the Memphis Belle."

"I've been doing a little flying myself," Gable said. "Stowing away on B-17s with a camera."

"I hear you flew five missions before they pulled the plug," Capra said.

"You heard right," Gable confirmed. "Got shot at twice and I guess that was too much for them. Now the only shooting I do is around a camera."

"They say you went up even when you didn't have to," Wyler said. "That you got so close to a ball turret gunner that you wanted to take over for him when he got killed, take over in every way."

"What's that supposed to mean?"

Wyler and Capra looked at each other as though they needed to draw straws. Capra took charge. "The rumor is you're trying to get yourself killed flying suicide missions."

"Horseshit!"

"You yourself said you didn't give a damn what happened to you after Carole died. What else can people think?"

Gable looked at Mavis. She couldn't help but have heard it. "People, maybe, but you know me better than that?"

"It's all over the Pentagon, Clark," Capra continued. "Hap Arnold himself is about to issue orders on top of grounding you but separating you from the service as a risk."

Gable set his jaw. "They can't do that! It's the only worthwhile thing I've done since Ma died."

Capra grew as serious as he'd ever been. He knew Gable, knew his thoughts. After all, he'd directed him to an Oscar. "Do you think your death will bring her back?"

Gable made a dismissive face. "C'mon, Frank, give me some credit."

"Convince me, Clark," Capra pushed. "I'll be the director, you be the actor."

Gable was having none of it. "Forget it! Life's hard enough. But y'know what I do think about? Sometimes I wonder what things'd be like if I never met Carol — what I'd be like if she'd never been born. Or what things'd be like if I'd never been born."

Capra considered this, then shook his head. "Never been born? That's the sappiest idea I ever heard."

Wyler, appearing sage, stepped into it. "I don't make Frank Copra pictures," he said softly in his German accent, "but if you ask me, maybe Clark doesn't have a death wish. Maybe he has a life wish. Maybe he's tempting the Grim Reaper as a way of celebrating life."

"You mean his desire to live is so great that he gives Death the razzberry?" Capra said, intrigued.

"Now you're talking."

"Is that some of that Freud malarkey?"

"Freud, schmoid," said Wyler, "the only question is, will it play in Peoria?"

Neither Wyler nor Capra noticed Gable take his leave. As he walked quietly away, he said to nobody in particular, "Good seeing you again, Frank. Nice meeting you, Willy. Please don't get up." He offered his arm to Mavis, she rose from her chair, and together they walked across the lobby toward the bar.

Wyler and Capra had a great deal to discuss. Like Gable, Wyler had taken to the air, not as a crew member but as a director. The Memphis Belle was a B-17 that had successfully flown twenty-five missions over occupied Europe between December of 1942 and May of 1943. Wyler had become intrigued with the combination of luck and skill of the plane and her crew and had been shooting color footage that he was assembling into a documentary much as we were putting together *Combat America*. What Wyler and Capra were trying to decide was whether to reveal that the footage in the film was not exclusively of the Memphis Belle but also of other bombers, and even other crews spliced together. In an effort to make the story cohesive and continuous, Wyler was going to combine material.

Capra, who headed the War Department's motion picture unit, was torn between good moviemaking and factual accuracy. At the same time, they wanted to create a legend that would inspire audiences. In fact, Wyler had informed the captain of the Belle that, if he had not returned from his final mission, the film would have been made anyway with another plane standing in for it. At least, this was the scuttlebutt I had been hearing around the editing room where we were finishing our picture. Like Gable, Wyler flew combat missions. Unlike Gable, he suffered injury. On one mission his flight was caught in aerial combat and he was exposed to such high noise levels that he lost his hearing and only partially recovered it. The resulting film, *The Memphis Belle: The Story of a Flying Fortress*, was the powerful sum of Wyler's wartime adventures. I hoped "Combat America" would be as prestigious for The King and I.

I thought about this as I returned to the base and went back to watching the rough cut of *Combat America* while lubricating myself with a bottle of gin procured on the way. You could get most anything you need in SoHo, including companionship, but the only company I wanted the way I was feeling was named Tanqueray.

Chapter 32

GABLE AND MAVIS PUSHED their un-sipped cocktails around the table top. The Dorchester was the perfect place for them to be talking. If Clark had ever considered taking her upstairs to the room he had optimistically reserved, everything he had told her so far that evening worked against using it. One of the quickest date-breakers is telling the woman you're with about the woman you're not with. Even a sympathetic ear such as Mavis was lending could take just so much competition from somebody who was not only not there, but was a saint.

"It wasn't just that Carole kept up with me on my outdoor stuff," Gable went on, "it was that she didn't mind pretending that she liked doing it. I know she would rather have been indoors decorating the house or playing cards, or out at the club or visiting friends. Instead, she made the peanut butter and jelly sandwiches and packed the hamper for our hunting trips. She trekked through the woods to the secret fishing holes and sat on wet sticks in the duck blinds. Do you know what would have happened to her career if she'd gotten her face scratched again? She already had a two-inch gash on her left cheek. They covered it with make-up and avoided cross-lighting, but you could still see it. It didn't make her any less beautiful and, you know what, she didn't demand to be filmed from just one side, like Colbert. She just went with the truth of it. That was Ma."

The lighting in the lounge was bright enough that everybody there could see it was Clark, yet the clientele was also bright and had the class not to bother him. As with the Maître D' s seating of us in the Grill, the advantage of billeting celebrities in luxury hotels is not simply so they can enjoy the posh surroundings but that other people who stay there, most of whom are also famous in their fields, know to respect their privacy.

"Does it help you to talk about her?" Mavis asked.

"I don't know," Gable said, "but I don't seem to be able to stop."

"How did you two meet?" Mavis asked.

"That doesn't help," he said, shaking his head. "That's an interview question. Thing is, I don't really want to talk about her, but I don't want to *not* talk about her, either. Does that make any sense?"

"How would you talk about her with one of the men you go hunting with? I'm sure they miss her, too."

"Talk about her with Hawks? With Fleming? No way. Funny. Fleming made *Gone with the Wind* with all those women and he never understood a one of them. When Harlow and I did *Red Dust*, he just told her 'action' and stood back. Yet women did some of their best work for him."

"I liked *Red Dust*," Mavis said.

"Funny thing happened there. We had a scene where Jean took a shower in a rain barrel. I don't think I ever met a woman who was more of a woman than her until Ma came along. So she finishes the scene and Vic calls 'cut' and Jean turns around and flashes those—" Gable looked around the hotel lounge and lowered his voice "—her bosom right at the camera and said, 'here's something for the film editors.' Do you know, Vic opened up the camera and ripped the raw film right out of the magazine and made her do it again — straight. That's how much he respected her — and didn't respect what someone else might do with the footage." Clark lowered his voice even more. "It was during that picture that Jean's husband, Paul Bern, killed himself. Poor kid. She really loved him. Nobody knows why he did it, either."

Mavis didn't say anything. She waited for Clark to talk again. When he did, he said, "I asked Alan before and I'll ask you now. Do you love him?"

"We're not here to talk about him."

"He has a name."

"All right, Alan. I don't know. What does it matter? There's a war on."

"Do you even like him?"

"Of course I do. But there's a war on."

"You don't love me, do you?" he said dismissively.

"That's the wrong question, Clark."

"There's no such thing as a wrong question."

"Yes there is, and you just asked it."

"I think you do love him and it bothers you to even think you could."

"I think you've got a hell of a nerve," Mavis said, getting up, taking her coat, and leaving. Gable threw a fiver on the table and lit off after her. By the time he got to the street, she had vanished into the night. He turned to the Doorman.

"The lady in a blue coat — which way did she go?"

"Toward Leicester Square, sir," he answered. Gable started walking. "No sir," the doorman said, "Leicester's the other way."

The August night was damp and chilly and seemed more so by the wartime blackout. Only the traffic lights worked, and they were muted. For a stranger trying to find his way around London without being able to see the street signs, it was an ordeal. Fortunately, everybody he stopped to ask directions knew who he was and had no hesitation helping.

"One block down and turn left, Mr. Gable."

"Another block over, Mr. Gable."

"Straight ahead, Clark, and what's your next picture?"

He turned the final corner but by then she had well and truly vanished. He found himself standing at the entrance of the Cat and Fiddle, a public house. Its windows were covered by curtains but a small, lighted sign in the door said "Open."

Chapter 33

TANQUERAY, SIEMENS, AND I were having a night of it. I watched the cut sequences of the film but found the projector increasingly unwilling to be threaded. Damn right I was drunk. I figured I was entitled. Wherever he was tonight, Clark was a grown-up. There was no way he could get lost in London, and if he was with Mavis, I had to throw in the towel. What can a guy do to win a girl if his competition is Clark Gable? I wished I had some tonic water. Did you ever stop to think that gin taste like disinfectant?

The movie played. It was the scene where the Eightball hit Antwerp, except you couldn't tell it was the Eightball, and it wasn't Antwerp, it was Schweinfurt. Or maybe it wasn't. Everything was edited together to look like one continuous raid, but I knew otherwise. The magic of film. What do you do if the editor wants the film one way, and you happen to want it another way?

"Ten thousand feet," Clark said in the voice-over, "low on oxygen. Check in your station. At the designated point, still in friendly territory, rendezvous with other groups. Your combat wing bangs into position. And wing after wing, as far as the eye can see, the attack forms. Heads for its assigned targets five hundred miles away.

Up until this moment, your fighter escort is still on the ground guarding his limited fuel capacity."

I had to admit, it was exciting. Sure, the camera work was shaky, and some of it was out of focus, and you could tell where they'd faked some of the action shots. But there was an authenticity about it that even the best Hollywood movies couldn't possibly muster. These were real guys flying real planes and shooting real ammo at real enemies who wanted to destroy everything we stood for, and only these men on the screen — not those who were safe back in Hollywood, but those I was watching — were doing the real job. Now I understood why Clark wanted to chuck the make-up and process screens and klieg lights and stunt men and artifice.

The end was particularly stirring: beauty shots of the planes and the men that flew them, and a shot of a plane's shadow across the ground, also known as a pilot's rainbow, heading home. Over this, Gable intoned — and there would be swelling music mixed in later — "Mission's end — but not the end of battle. Fighting men from Maine to California will have a long, tough rainbow to travel. But they're looking the enemy right between his eyes. They're fighting in the American way — their American way of life — enemies of America, look at these men. They're not gonna lose, brother."

With Tanqueray's coaching, I started to ad lib my own narration, which I thought was better: "And so, as the Third Reich sinks slowly in the east, we say goodbye to the brave crew of the Eightball. Goodbye to Elizabeth the gauze-wrapper. Goodbye to the asshole drill sergeant. Goodbye to Mavis Roberts and the fence she's sitting on. And hello to the front lines where we are about to get our big, comfortable, Hollywood asses shot off."

I heard applause. Two huge shadows appeared on the screen. They had smooth, round heads. My eyes adjusted and saw that they were helmeted MPs blocking the projector's light beam.

"Lieutenant Greenberg?" one of them said.

Meanwhile Gable's voice was still saying, "The ball turret gunner is the point man on these runs. He's got his finger on the trigger — the best seat in the whole theatre — the European theatre, that is."

The other MP turned on the room light and cut the projector. It grumbled to a stop.

"Are you Lieutenant Alan Greenberg?" the first MP asked.

"He's out," I said, hoisting the half-empty bottle, "or he soon will be."

The second MP had no sense of humor. "Front and center!"

I stumbled to my feet and, in the process, almost fell over. The first MP didn't have a sense of humor, either.

"What do you have to say for yourself?" he demanded.

What could I say? I cradled the gin bottle like an Oscar and said, "I'd like to thank the Academy — "

The first MP snatched it from my hand and chucked it into a wire trash can. By then the second MP had hoisted me over his shoulder and we were heading out of the screening room. The next thing I remember was being hit full-on by a cold shower.

Chapter 34

"Your friend Gable," the first MP said as he yanked me from under the cold water nozzle, "had a six-hour pass and he hasn't shown up. That means he's AWOL. The Colonel wants him here and now, and you're one of two people who always know where he is. So where is he?"

"What am I, his baby sitter?" I asked, shaking off the wetness.

"That's what they say," the second MP said as he and the first one handed me a towel and aimed me toward dry clothes. "So you're gonna lead us to him and it we don't find him, we're putting you in the brig instead."

I got dressed groggily and by the time I was sober enough to think straight, I was riding into town with them in the back of a sedan.

"Don't you guys use Jeeps?" I asked.

"Low profile," the one who was driving said. "The Colonel wants Captain Gable, not major scandal." I ignored his attempt at a pun.

"Wait a minute," I suddenly realized, "you said two people. Who's the other one?"

The second MP said, "Colonel Hatcher's civilian adjutant. Miss Mavis Roberts signed out on the duty roster that she and Gable were going to the Dorchester Hotel. The Dorchester doorman says that they went their separate ways hours ago, and we can't find either one of them, so we came and got you."

"Can you imagine that?" the driver said. "What dame in her right mind would run out on Clark Gable? Somebody tell me."

"How much time do you have?" I said.

"Anyway," the one riding shotgun went on, "we'll swing by her apartment. None of these Brits have their own phones, so we'll take a chance."

"She has a roommate," the driver said. "Maybe she knows something."

"That depends on how interested you are in gauze," I said.

When we got to the flat, I rushed inside, girding for Elizabeth. I was surprised when Mavis answered.

"What are you doing here?" she asked.

"What are *you* doing here?" I answered. Then she saw the MPs. "I brought a couple of friends," I said. "They were looking for Clark and why aren't you still with him?"

"Do we have to talk in the hallway?" Mavis said. "Come in."

"With all due respect, ma'am," the first MP said, "Why don't you put on a jacket and help us find him."

"What for?" asked Mavis as she grabbed her wrap and descended the stairs with us. "I can't imagine he's had time to do anything."

"He's overstayed a six-hour pass and technically he's absent without leave," the MP continued. We've been dispatched by Colonel Hatcher to bring him back before some real MPs find him and mark him for Court Martial.

"Court-Martialed for being late?" I said.

"In time of war," the second MP said grimly, "anything goes."

"Can't you cut him some slack?" I asked.

"We're the slack. We just wear these uniforms. We're Hatcher's orderlies."

Mavis finally spoke. "I don't want to go into our conversation in the hotel, but I left heading west and he didn't catch up with me, so he must have gone in another direction."

"What was his mood?" the second MP asked.

"He had a lot on his mind," Mavis replied diplomatically.

I broke the code. "He means was he drunk or sober?"

"Sober." She said. "Very sober. Too sober, in fact."

"I think you owe it to me to tell me how you left it," I said directly.

"Left what?" she said.

"Don't be coy," I said. "How did he leave the two of you. For that matter, how did *you* leave the two of you?"

"He left it by leaving," she said, then to nobody in particular. "I don't know myself."

"Does this help us find him any faster?" the first MP asked.

"How should I know?" I said angrily, still trying to untangle Mavis and Clark in my mind. "I'll help as much as I can, but I don't know the town well enough to find Buckingham Palace if the King himself needed directions. Why even drag me along?"

The first MP looked at me like I was an idiot. "Because he's your responsibility, According to everyone on the base, you're guarding Gable."

Chapter 35

ALL MY TIME IN England I wanted to do a pub crawl. That's where you visit a string of pubs with your mates (friends) consuming one pint in each of them and going on to the next one and the next one until you either pass out or reach closing time. Many consider it a ritual, a rite of passage. As much as I wanted to do one, I had never considered doing it with a woman and two MPs. What made this pub crawl more awkward is that none of us touched a drop.

The pub, or public house, is one of the grandest English traditions. In neighborhoods, the "local" is where friends gather during strictly regulated hours of operation that are designed not to conflict with dinner or church. Many are divided into bar and tables: the bar side is where men drink and smoke, and the table half is where women and families sit. Compared with American neighborhood taverns, British pubs feel more convivial; although people come to both places to drink, there appears to be a pub society unlike that in America. People know each other and take notice of strangers. Just as in the gothic horror films when everyone in the pub grows quiet and stares at newcomers who enter off the moors, we were counting on pub patrons to recognize a movie star when he paid them a visit.

Because if Clark wasn't on the base and hadn't started drinking, we had the whole City of London to try to find him in.

The Bubble and Squeak, which I learned was named after what people called yesterday's leftovers all crushed in a frying pan and served today, hadn't seen him. Neither had The King's Whistle, The Snake and Apple, or The Hunting Monk. That last one distinguished itself in my memory by having a walk-down entrance with a warning sign mounted on a crossbeam that read "duck or grouse" lest you hit your head going in.

Mavis and I managed to persuade the MPs to stay in the car while we went into the Cock and Bull. We were beginning to get the feeling that Clark had climbed on the wagon when the barmaid said, "As a matter of fact, he was in here an hour ago, had a pint of bitters, then saw something in the newspaper and left in a hurry."

"Do you still have the newspaper?" I asked. She gave it to me. Mavis and I flipped through the pages.

"Do you think he saw something? she asked.

"He must have," I said. "But what?"

The *Times* contained the usual war reports, feature stories on fifty ways to disguise potatoes, a list of razed buildings and street closings, and profiles of men and women in service. Nothing out of the ordinary or that might appeal to a visiting Yank.

"Any idea what he saw right before he bolted?" I asked. The barmaid shook her head No and went back to pulling pints.

"Let's use our brains," Mavis said. "You're both in the movie business. What do you look at first when you get the papers?"

I hated myself. "The obits," I admitted. "Then the current movie section." We turned to the cinema listings. "Where's the best place to find a movie star?"

Mavis and I said it at the same time: "In the movies."

We dashed from the pub and dove into the sedan. "Get to the Odeon Leicester Square," Mavis told the driver. "It's our best bet."

A jaunt through the sparse nighttime war traffic and we were there. The marquee lights were out but the poster cases were still illuminated even thought the box office was closed after the last show had begun. The attraction was *To Be or Not to Be*, Carole Lombard's last film.

The movie was a huge gamble for director Ernst Lubitsch and producer Alexander Korda. Lombard and Jack Benny starred as a husband-and-wife acting team with a Polish theatre troupe in occupied Poland. Plot contrivances force them to become involved with impersonating a brutal Nazi commander and the scheme almost falls apart over Benny's intense jealousy of anybody who looks at his lovely wife. Making a comedy about Nazis was brave enough when Charlie Chaplin did it in *The Great Dictator* in 1940, but by the time Lubitsch and Korda made *To Be or Not to Be* in 1942 the world had heard of the concentration camps and Hitler was anything but funny. Released in the spring of that year, it was apparently playing a reissue engagement at the Odeon, and we took a chance that Clark would be drawn to it. I asked Mavis to wait in the lobby while I went into the auditorium to search for Clark.

English theatres are scaled by ticket price. I looked in the posh seats first, then the cheap ones, trying to see through the darkness and the cigarette smoke, which was permitted at the time. There were only a handful of patrons, none of them Clark. Then I happened to stare up and see that the theatre had a balcony. I found the stairs and went up. It was empty except for one person, and that one person was Clark. I sat beside him, asking. "Is this seat taken?"

He kept staring at the movie. I used the light reflecting off the screen to try and read his face. The scene was between Benny, Lombard, and Henry Victor playing a Gestapo officer. Lombard's character had to placate Schultz, but Benny's jealous egocentric interference put her in danger and the plan in doubt. Typical for Lubitsch, there were three or four threads going at the same time, all of them brilliantly balanced and expertly played.

Clark smiled as he watched Carole work. Finally he turned his head to me with his eyes still fixed on the screen, and said, "God, she was the best."

He looked at his hands, which were folded in his lap.

"All my life, I used older women. They made me Clark Gable. When the public made me famous, the studio made me the King. Then there were the agents, the fan magazines — " He looked at me. "— the publicists. Can you imagine how strange that sounds: 'The King'?

"It was always other people, other people always wanting a piece of you. Ma was the first one who didn't want anything, and that's why I gave her everything, starting with my heart. I was just a big lug on the screen until I met her. Carole gave me confidence."

I'd never had anybody open up to me like this, not even old girlfriends. If Mavis was right — that guys can't open up to guys — what was Clark doing saying this to me? Then he stopped talking like it was now my turn.

"I know you don't like me much," I started, "and, when you think about it, this whole thing is pretty weird. I mean the way they made me join up to keep watch on you."

"I don't think you're so bad, Junior," he said. "You take a punch okay."

"Let me finish," I said, "because I don't think we're ever going to be in this mood at the same time again. I just want you to know that thanks to you I've learned to cut through the Hollywood bullshit and see the real person inside. Now I think I begin to understand what you have to go through, and how you needed someone like Miss Lombard — who also had to put up with it — to share the craziness. Whatever happens from now on — if I get reassigned, fired, killed, or whatever — thank you for being Clark Gable with me and not the King."

"That's good, Junior. I don't drop my guard that often. Now let's talk about you.

"Me? What's there to talk about?"

"That girl likes you, you know."

"She has a funny way of showing it."

"She will show it if you show it first."

"What do you think I've been doing for the last year?"

"You push too hard. Stand still and let her come to you. I promise you she will."

"What if you're wrong? How do you tell if a girl really likes you?"

"Are you kidding? I'm Clark Gable." He smiled the Gable smile and I figured he was kidding, so I laughed, too. He dropped his smile and grabbed my arm. "You know the toughest line any actor has to say on screen?"

"I give up."

"I love you."

"I love you, too, Clark, but we have to get back to the base. There's a couple of MPs in the lobby waiting to take us."

"The line of *dialogue*, Junior. 'I love you' is the hardest thing to say."

"Is it any easier to say it in real life?" I asked.

Gable stared at me. "Try it some time."

We walked downstairs to the lobby. I wondered what anybody leaving the cinema early would have thought if they left the auditorium and ran into Clark Gable. The lobby was darkened in preparation for closing as soon as the show was over. The MPs were waiting there for Clark.

"Hi, fellas," he said buoyantly. "Can I buy you a drink?"

"Captain," the first MP said, " it is my duty to inform you that you are Absent Without Leave and we have to place you under arrest."

"Hey," I said, "what are you talking about? You said you wouldn't arrest him."

"Would you have helped us find him if we hadn't promised?" the second MP said.

I was angry. "I'll take this all the way up to Colonel Hatcher."

"Fine," the MP said. "You get one phone call from the brig."

Gable easily put the pieces together. "Hold it, hold it, fellas," he said. "Leave this kid out of it. I'm wrong. I needed some time to think so I skipped out on the pass. I'll go quietly." He held out his wrists to be cuffed.

"That won't be necessary, Captain," the second MP said.

"Okay, but just one thing." He played to me. "I was a heel tonight with someone we both know, a good kid who deserves someone better than me. You follow?"

"I think I do," I said.

Clark kicked me in the rump. "Now do something about it!"

As if on cue, Mavis stepped out of the shadows. Gable looked at her but kept talking to me. "And if the two of you don't do something about it, then you're saps and I wash my hands of the both of you."

"Wait a minute," the second MP said, "Isn't that from *It Happened One Night?*"

Gable ignored him. "You got your wish, Junior. No more combat missions. If you need me for publicity in the future, I'll be in the brig." Then he turned to the MPs. "Okay, boys, let's go."

"Just a moment," I said. "I think I can help. Okay, so the Captain's AWOL. And maybe a little insubordinate. And he's wasted our time and energy looking for him all over town."

"Try not to help me so much," Gable stage-whispered.

"Maybe we can work something out. After all, no real harm has been done, right? Colonel Hatcher certainly isn't pacing the floor waiting for the Captain to show up. We have a little time to fix things." I sidled toward the MPs. "You're movie fans. You recognized 'It Happened One Night.' We have the biggest star in the world standing here. Maybe your sweethearts want an autograph, or your mothers. Maybe you know someone else who does."

I stepped even closer to the MPs and gave them my own stage whisper. "Some guys even sell autographs like his for ten bucks apiece."

The MPs didn't budge. Would you believe that? Honest MPs. So Mavis took matters into her practiced, military-trained hands. "If you don't accept the autographs," she said, "I shall tell Colonel Hatcher that you did. And then you will be in the brig instead of Clark."

The second MP was the first to crack. "You mean his actual signature? On real photographs?"

I nodded yes. The first MP also agreed. "You've got a deal. When do we get them?"

"How many do you want, fellas?" I asked. "I will take care of it personally."

Chapter 36

PETROL RATIONING BEING WHAT it was and the hour being close to midnight in a completely blacked-out London with curfews in place, we all piled into the sedan for the MPs to drop us home. Somehow Clark managed to sit between Mavis and me making the back of the car a comfortable place to carry on an uncomfortable conversation.

"The last time the three of us were together it didn't turn out too well," Clark said with unexpected cheeriness. "If I recall, you, Mavis, were trying to get rid of Junior, and Junior wanted to get rid of me. How did that end up? Oh, that's right. Mavis wound up getting rid of me."

Mavis and I rode in silence.

"I think you're a swell girl, Mavis. I really do. In fact, you remind me a lot of the women I fell in love with before Carole came along." He elbowed me to make sure I remembered what he'd told me. "And, Junior, you remind me of the people at the studio who try to protect me because they like me and not just because it's their job. There aren't a lot of them." He must have elbowed Mavis for a similar reason because I saw her jump. "Now it's you kids' turn to say why you like each other. I'll just shut my yap."

Crickets.

"I see where this is going," Gable continued after an uneasy silence, "which is nowhere. Junior, you've been on Mavis's tail ever since you thought she was horning onto your territory, right? C'mon, Junior, answer me."

"Yes, but I understand that's her job."

"Mavis, you've had a problem with Junior looking over your shoulder all the time, haven't you?"

"Yes," Mavis said without adding anything.

"Since the two of you have so much in common, why don't I just back out of this and let you work it out."

"I don't understand," said Mavis. I was starting to, however.

"Say, Jeeves," Gable told the MP who was driving, "turn this jalopy around and head back to the Dorchester, wouldja? If there's a problem with that, consider it an order."

"Sorry, sir, but you're due on the base."

"Oh, I intend to go back to the base with you. But, see, I still have a suite reserved at the Dorchester, and these two reluctant lovebirds could use it more than I can. What do you think?"

"I like your style, Captain," the driver said, turning the car around and heading back into town.

"Whose name is the room under?" I asked.

"Well, it ain't Greta Garbo," Gable said. Then he eyed me suspiciously. "Although by the time the studio gets the room service bill, it probably will be, eh? What do you say, Junior?"

"Captain Gable," I said, "do you think just once you could call me Alan?"

He laughed, punched me gently on the cheek, and didn't call me Alan. When we got back to the Dorchester, the doorman let us out of the car. I went around to the curb side and took Mavis's hand. "Well, Greta," I said, "do you vant to be alone?"

Mavis raised an eyebrow. "Not tonight, I don't."

Gable stayed in the car. "Alan!" he called out.

I turned around to see him throw me a salute. I returned it.

"You're okay, Junior," he said as the doorman closed the door and he drove off with the MPs.

When Mavis checked in with Colonel Hatcher in the morning she was relieved to find that the AWOL order had been rescinded and that all the Colonel wanted to talk to Gable about was recording more narration for *Combat America*. "The Colonel gets excitable sometimes," she explained.

Clark was indeed grounded permanently in late September of 1943 under the reasoning that he was too important to place in jeopardy, patriotism or not. In May of 1944 he was promoted to the rank of major, and on June 12 he was allowed to resign from the service. The official reason was his age (forty-three) but, in reality, he felt useless in his *de facto* public relations capacity when what he had always wanted to do was fight Hitler. By that time, of course — D-Day plus six — the job of fighting Hitler was winding down. He was awarded the Air Medal and the Distinguished Flying Cross.

As for *Combat America*, Clark was allowed to finish it but the film was never widely shown. Conceived and produced as a recruitment tool, by the time it was ready for release the air war was almost over and flyers were no longer needed. Its air drama was dwarfed by William Wyler's "Memphis Belle" and it exists today as a curiosity, albeit a notable one.

Clark returned to America and began working again at Metro-Goldwyn-Mayer where he was immediately put into a picture called

Adventure opposite Greer Garson, the acclaimed star of the uplifting wartime drama, *Mrs. Miniver*. The picture was famously advertised with the slogan, "Gable's Back and Garson's Got Him!" The studio figured that Gable could appear in anything and a hungry public would buy tickets. When Mr. Mayer and the MGM brass got a look at it, however, they had second thoughts.

"Clark goes off to fight a war and he comes back to *this* dreck?" Mr. Mayer roared when the lights came up. "He goes away for four years, fights Hitler, gets shot at with real bullets, and the first movie he makes, he falls for a — a *librarian*? Fire the writer."

"That'd be hard to do, L.B.," Sam Marx, the studio story editor, said. "We had twelve of them working on it. If we fire the writer, we lose our whole writing staff."

"*Twelve writers?*" Mayer ranted, turning red. "Moses wrote the first five books of the old Testament alone, for Christ's sake! And he wasn't even union."

"The public is ready for anything Clark Gable is in, L.B.," Howard Strickling said calmly, hoping it would bring Mayer's blood pressure down. "In fact, they're so Gable-hungry that David Selznick is pushing us to reissue *Gone with the Wind*."

"Plus we're already shooting *The Hucksters*, Eddie Mannix said. "That's a great script and only three writers worked on it."

Mayer started reciting the picture's catch-phrase. "Gable's back and Garson's got him. Gable's back and Garson's got him." I like it. Whose idea was it?

"Alan Greenberg," Strickling answered.

"Fire him," Mayer commanded.

"Excuse me?" said Strickling.

"Fire him. He was supposed to protect Clark and he almost got him killed. That kind of protection I don't need. While you're at it, make sure he doesn't work anywhere else in this town."

"But L.B.," Mannix said. "Greenberg's a war hero. He was shot at, just like Clark."

"I don't care," Mayer decreed. "So Hitler didn't get him. I will."

"Well, I care." The voice came from inside the projection booth. The man who said it left the booth, stepped onto the outdoor cat-walk, and into the door of the screening room, letting in light that blinded the executives.

It was Clark. Mr. Mayer turned on a dime. "Clark!" he said joyously. "We've got a hell of a trailer for this picture. Have you seen it? You were never better!"

"Shut up, L.B.," he said. There were audible hemorrhages from everyone in the room. "I heard everything. I also found out how many strings you pulled trying to keep me out of the service, and how you blackmailed Alan into coming along."

Even caught by surprise, Mayer had the stature to stand up to his star. "It was for your own good, Clark, and the good of Metro."

"Ha!" Gable laughed in Mayer's face. "It was for your own personal good, L.B. I know the fights you have with Nick Schenck back in New York. If you really cared about me and Metro you'd slice this piece of shit into guitar picks."

"That Greenberg kid's only job was to keep you out of harm's way. You could've been killed."

"There's lots of ways to keep somebody alive, L.B.," Clark said, looking at Mannix, Strickling, and Marx. "The best way is to make 'em want to keep living. I owe Greenberg that, and so do you. If he hadn't been there — as a person, not as a studio — I don't know what I would have done. It took me a long time to see that. But thanks to him, I did."

Mannix stepped up. "Is this your way of starting contract talks, Clark? You want more money?"

"No, I don't want more money, Eddie. But I'll tell you what I do want. I want Alan Greenberg to be my personal publicist as long as I'm under contract here. Just like Otto Winkler was. He'll report to me, not to you."

"That can be done," Mayer said, "and good riddance."

"And one more thing," Clark said. "As long as you like to pull strings, I've got one or two that I'd like you to pull for me. And they're a deal-breaker."

Gable stared at Mayer's cold eyes with every molecule of menace he could muster as an actor and as a man, for he knew it was the only way to force the most powerful man in Hollywood to deliver the goods.

Chapter 37

ADVENTURE PLAYED AS POORLY on the big screen as it had in its private showing at MGM but the public didn't care. Gable was Gable, and even after four years away from theatres he was the draw that Metro counted on to pull them through until *The Hucksters* was ready. Truth to tell, Clark went into *Adventure* with his eyes open. He wanted to work, he knew he had to in order to sustain his career, and he gambled that, with a dozen talented writers all working behind each other on the admittedly slim story, enough would come out of it that his old pal Victor Fleming could make into a picture.

But Fleming was having a rough time, too. The versatile workhorse who had directed both *The Wizard of Oz* and *Gone with the Wind* at practically the same time lost his muse after the war. *Adventure* was his last film for Metro after a career that he had begun there in the early 30s. Suddenly independent and without the MGM machine behind him, he almost killed himself pulling together *Joan of Arc*, starring Ingrid Bergman, with whom he was having an affair, and produced by Walter Wanger, with whom he was having a fight.

Gable survived *Adventure*, but I very nearly didn't. I saw it once at a studio screening and then decided to see it again with my new wife. It was an ordeal. After the show broke, while waiting for her to visit the ladies room, I haunted the lobby of the Loew's theatre listening for clues from departing patrons about Clark's durability.

"Well, he's still the King as far as I'm concerned," said one middle-aged lady who was leaving with her friend, also a middle-aged lady, who agreed that "he still looks good!"

"I wonder if anything happened to him in the war," the first one mused.

"Such as?" asked the second.

"Well, whenever my daughter asks my son-in-law what it was like in battle, he clams up. Do you think Clark had the same experience?"

"Gable in battle?" her friend said. "You know how they protect all the famous people. That story about him getting shot at over Belgium? Pure publicity."

"But I read it in the fan magazine," the first one said. "It has to be true!"

I had to smile at their gullibility. No, *gullibility* is a cruel word. Let's say that I had to smile at how they hooked their hearts onto the dreams that we created for them.

While I was patting myself and my profession on the back, my wife arrived. "Took you long enough," I said with a smile.

"Back home we have proper powder rooms."

"Okay, then," I challenged, "you want to go back?"

"Not after Mr. Mayer practically threw himself at President Truman's feet to get me here as a war bride," she said. "Perhaps we can go back on business some time."

"Only if Clark makes a picture there," I said. "But I'll work on it." Then I bit the bullet. "What did you think of the picture?"

"I much preferred Greer Garson in *Mrs. Miniver*, my wife said. "But her handsome co-star — what's his name?"

"Clark Gable," I smiled at our private joke. "I hear he's a big star. What do you think of him?

"Oh, he's all right," my wife — Mavis — smiled back. "But he's no Alan Greenberg."

In 1949, Clark did go back to England. He married Lady Sylvia Ashley. They divorced in 1952 and in 1955 he married Kay Williams. They say he never loved another woman the way he had loved Carole.

People have asked what made Clark Gable so special. Surely there were other male stars of his era who were just as big: Spencer Tracy, Gary Cooper, Humphrey Bogart, Errol Flynn, Cary Grant, James Stewart, Henry Fonda — the list is long and rich. Each possessed the qualities of masculinity, intelligence, world-weariness, adventure, and self-effacing good humor that made him appealing to men as well as women. As famous as they were, you could easily imagine having a beer with them. They were real. Notably, they were all from the old school of acting where they just came in and did it. None of that method stuff where acting includes letting the audience know you're acting. As James Cagney — also one of the greats — said of the craft he mastered, "Learn your lines, find your mark, look 'em in the eye, and tell 'em the truth."

What distinguished the great stars is that they had personalities. You know they lived their lives as big off the screen as on it, and they brought the reality of their experience to their roles. When

Spencer Tracy played a priest, you knew he used his Catholic guilt to enrich his portrayal. Gary Cooper was a real cowboy before he became the screen's quintessential one. Humphrey Bogart, although raised in luxury, led a rough-and-tumble life that toughened for his screen roles. Everybody knew that Errol Flynn was a rogue in three countries before he arrived in Hollywood. Cary Grant was a fabrication who became, on the screen, everything he always wanted to be as Archie Leech. James Stewart steeled himself as a combat pilot to become the grizzled eminence that earned him immortality. And Henry Fonda called upon his Nebraska honesty to play presidents and commanders that were just as trusted as his American roots.

Gable wasn't selected for stardom by Hollywood. It was the public that did it. Before *The Painted Desert* in 1931 he had worked as an extra, but his portrayal of the nasty, vindictive Rance Brett opposite William Boyd in a contrived story about two feuding ranchers brought him his first fan mail. It could easily have been that he was the only interesting character in the histrionic piece. It could also have been that he simply had that indefinable something that makes stars. When it happens, you know it. Someone walks on the screen and suddenly there's nobody else there.

Likewise, when Gable walked into a room, the walls moved back. He was taller than most actors — six foot one. His head was also slightly larger and wider than most people's, which, incidentally, is remarkably common for stars, and it has nothing to do with ego. Perhaps it's the slightly enlarged features that draw attention on a movie screen. In any event, it worked for Clark, and his larger-than-life personality filled in the corners.

The most obvious part of Clark's talent is that, when you watched him on the screen, you just knew that he wanted to be there. Even if the picture was bad, Gable wasn't. He always found a way to appear to be enjoying himself, and it was infectious, not only with the audience but with everyone who worked with him. You never heard bad things about Gable, even whispered on the lot. This says more about the man than any award he ever received.

His death in 1960 was a blow not only to those of us who knew him but to the screen's image of the American male. He was only 59 but he had romanced, if you can imagine it, three generations of screen women from Garbo to Joan Crawford to Barbara Stanwyck to Jean Harlow to Grace Kelley to Vivien Leigh to Doris Day and, finally, to Marilyn Monroe. It was Monroe's tardiness on the location where John Huston was shooting *The Misfits* that they say did Gable in. Always prompt and prepared, he simmered when Monroe was neither. When it came time to shoot a scene where his character, rancher Gay Langland, had to rope and break a wild horse on the scorching desert of Stagecoach, Nevada, he insisted on doing it himself rather than yield the grueling task to a stunt actor. The physical stress, on top of the emotional turmoil, gave him the heart attack that killed him on November 16, 1960, not long after the picture wrapped.

He had everything to live for; Kay Williams, his wife since 1955, was about to produce a child. John Clark Gable, Clark's only son, was born on March 20, 1961. It's sad that the boy never knew his father except as the man that the world loved on the screen. Then, again, from what I would see of the kid on the occasional TV interview, he was doing his father proud. He even had a son, Clark James Gable — Clark's grandson — who entered acting.

When Clark died, I retired from publicity and became a writer specializing in Hollywood's unknown history, such as the story you have just read.

Nat Segaloff (Author)

Nat Segaloff is a writer-producer-journalist. He covered the film industry for *The Boston Herald*, but has also variously been a studio publicist (Fox, UA, Columbia), college teacher (Boston University, Boston College), and broadcaster (Group W, CBS, Storer). He is the author of sixteen books including *Hurricane Billy: The Stormy Life and Films of William Friedkin*, *Arthur Penn: American Director*, and *Final Cuts: The Last Films of 50 Great Directors* in addition to career monographs on Stirling Silliphant, Walon Green, Paul Mazursky and John Milius. His writing has appeared in such varied periodicals as *Film Comment, Written By, International Documentary, Animation Magazine, The Christian Science Monitor, Time Out* (US), *MacWorld*, and *American Movie Classics Magazine*. He was also senior reviewer for AudiobookCafe.com and contributing writer to *Moving Pictures* magazine. His *The Everything® Etiquette Book* and *The Everything Trivia Book* and *The Everything® Tall Tales, Legends & Outrageous Lies Book* were best-sellers for Adams Media Corp.

As a TV writer-producer, Segaloff helped perfect the format and create episodes for A&E's flagship *Biography* series. His distinctive productions include episodes on John Belushi, Stan Lee, Larry King, Shari Lewis & Lamb Chop, and Darryl F. Zanuck.

He wrote and co-produced the *Rock 'n' Roll Moments* music series for The Learning Channel/Malcolm Leo Productions, and has written and/or produced programming for New World, Disney, Turner Classic Movies, and USA Networks. He is co-creator/co-producer of *Judgment Day* with Gayle Kirschenbaum and Grosso-Jacobson Communications Corp. for HBO.

His extraterrestrial endeavors include the cheeky sequel to the Orson Welles "Invasion From Mars" radio hoax, "When Welles Collide," which featured a "Star Trek"® cast. It was produced by L.A. Theatre Works and has become a Halloween tradition on National Public Radio. In 1996 he formed the multi-media production company Alien Voices® with actors Leonard Nimoy and John de Lancie and produced five best-selling, fully dramatized audio plays for Simon & Schuster: *The Time Machine, Journey to the Center of the Earth, The Lost World, The Invisible Man* and *The First Men in the Moon,* all of which featured "Star Trek"® casts. Additionally, his teleplay for *The First Men in the Moon* was the first-ever TV/Internet simulcast and was presented live on The Sci-Fi Channel. He has also written a narrative concert for the Los Angeles Philharmonic, special material for celebrity fundraising events, is a script consultant, and is a frequent contributor to Nikki Finke's celebrated Hollywood fiction website, HollywoodDementia.com

Nat is the co-author (with Daniel M. Kimmel and Arnie Reisman) of *The Waldorf Conference,* a comedy-drama about the secret 1947 meeting of studio moguls that began the Hollywood Blacklist, which had its all-star world premiere at L.A. Theatre Works. and was acquired for production by Warner Bros. He produced a subsequent production to benefit the Hollywood ACLU and the Writers Guild Foundation, and has also produced such other celebrity events as a public reading of censored books and a recreation of the classic anti-HUAC broadcast, "Hollywood Fights Back." He was staff producer for The Africa Channel, wrote the stage play *Closets* (produced at Massachusetts' Gloucester Stage Company), and was writer for the popular public radio word/game show "Says You!" after having been a frequent guest panelist.

His biography *A Lit Fuse: The Provocative Life of Harlan Ellison* (NESFA Press) was nominated for Hugo and Locus awards. Previous books for Bear Manor Media include *Stirling Silliphant: The Fingers of God; Mr. Huston/Mr. North: Life, Death, and the Making of John Huston's Last Film;* and *Screen Saver: Private Stories of Public Hollywood,* its sequel, *Screen Saver Too: Hollywood Strikes Back* and, with Yoram Ben-Ami, *Guiding Royalty: My Adventure with Elizabeth Taylor and Richard Burton.* He also records the audiobook editions of many of his and other books which are released by through Bear Manor Audio and Blackstone Audio. His audiobook for *Guarding Gable* is enhanced with sound effects and dialogue from the actual films Gable made during the war.

His next project is the biography of Shari Lewis and Lamb Chop.

Nat lives in Los Angeles and really tries to return phone calls. His website is www.NatSegaloff.com

www.ingramcontent.com/pod-product-compliance
Lightning Source LLC
Chambersburg PA
CBHW071830020726
47502CB00004B/1298